FOUNTAINVILLE

i.m.
John Emrys Roberts and Blodwen Griffiths

TISHANI DOSHI

FOUNTAINVILLE

NEW STORIES FROM THE
MABINOGION

SEREN

Seren is the book imprint of
Poetry Wales Press Ltd
57 Nolton Street, Bridgend, Wales, CF31 3AE
www.serenbooks.com

ISBN 978-1-78172-108-7
ebook ISBN 978-1-78172-110-0

Cover design by Mathew Bevan

Inner design and typesetting by books@lloydrobson.com

Printed by TJ International, Cornwall

The publisher acknowledges the financial support of the
Welsh Books Council.

MIX
Paper from
responsible sources
FSC
www.fsc.org   FSC® C013056

Contents

New Stories from the Mabinogion

Introduction

Some stories, it seems, just keep on going. Whatever you do to them, the words are still whispered abroad, a whistle in the reeds, a bird's song in your ear.

Every culture has its myths; many share ingredients with each other. Stir the pot, retell the tale and you draw out something new, a new flavour, a new meaning maybe. There's no one right version. Perhaps it's because myths were a way of describing our place in the world, of putting people and their search for meaning in a bigger picture, that they linger in our imagination.

The eleven stories of the *Mabinogion* ('story of youth') are diverse native Welsh tales taken from two medieval manuscripts. But their roots go back hundreds of years, through written fragments and the unwritten, storytelling tradition. They were first collected under this title, and translated into English, in the nineteenth century.

The *Mabinogion* brings us Celtic mythology, Arthurian romance, and a history of the Island of Britain seen through the eyes of medieval Wales – but tells tales that stretch way beyond the boundaries of contemporary Wales, just as the 'Welsh' part of this island once did: Welsh was once spoken as far north as Edinburgh. In one tale, the gigantic Bendigeidfran wears the crown of London, and his severed head is buried there, facing France, to protect the land from invaders.

There is enchantment and shape-shifting, conflict, peacemaking, love, betrayal. A wife conjured out of flowers is punished for unfaithfulness by being turned into an owl, Arthur and his knights chase a magical wild boar and its piglets from Ireland across south Wales to Cornwall, a prince changes places with the king of the underworld for a year...

Many of these myths are familiar in Wales, and some have filtered through into the wider British tradition, but others are little known beyond the Welsh border. In this series of New Stories from the Mabinogion the old tales are at the heart of the new, to be enjoyed wherever they are read.

Each author has chosen a story to reinvent and retell for their own reasons and in their own way: creating fresh, contemporary tales that speak to us as much of the world we know now as of times long gone.

Penny Thomas, series editor

Fountainville

A Little Fable

'Alas,' said the mouse, 'the world is growing smaller every day. At first it was so big that I was afraid, I ran on and I was glad when at last I saw walls to left and right of me in the distance, but these long walls are closing in on each other so fast that I have already reached the end room, and there in the corner stands the trap that I am heading for.' 'You only have to change direction,' said the cat, and ate it up.

Franz Kafka, *The Great Wall of China and Other Short Works*

Part One

I

People know our town because of the fountain. For centuries, grannies and god-men have been saying, *Go to Fountainville*. Go to Fountainville, and you'll be cured of all your problems. Arrive there barren, tired, deprived, mad, washed inside out with nowhere else to go, and you might be restored. They've been spinning stories from the beginning, of course, about places that are holier than others – villages along riverbanks where it's auspicious to die, citadels where eternal flames burn, pilgrim centres to heal your heart. In the old myths and the new, there have always been places with special powers, and Fountainville is such a place.

Not that our town looks very different from any others in these Borderlands. There are good parts and bad, same as the rest, and it doesn't take very long to figure out which side's which. The dangerous folk stick to the west for the brothels, opium dens and gambling saloons, and the pious circumambulate the east where the school, church and clinic are set up. Only the stray dogs and roosters roam freely across both sides, paying no heed to who is watching who.

Main Street, which divides Fountainville, is a dirty narrow road with stores on either side that cramp up on each other, where you can procure everything from king chillies to imported silk shirts. Those who can't afford to rent a space bring their wares and spread themselves out on the stone blocks above the sewers to chew on tobacco and gossip. Further up the street are government offices, tearooms and the newly established Sanity Boarding House – the only place for out-of-towners to stay. At the very top of the street is the bus station and the cinema, which can always be relied upon to play one of those song-and-dance films they produce on the Mainland. A few years ago, in a bid to offer 'positive outlets' to our disenchanted youth, the municipality installed the Ambition Computer Centre and a bodybuilding gym beside the cinema so our youngsters could aspire to look like those gyrating muscleheads in the films.

Most of the townsfolk of Fountainville are farmers who cultivate rice and rapeseed, millet and maize, still using bullocks as their ancestors did a hundred years ago. They live in simple mud houses with tin roofs on the outskirts of the Northern Forest Ridge. The only signs of prosperity there are the outcrops of television satellite dishes that stick out of every roof, forming strange mushroom shapes against the sky. The rich, of which there are few – government officials, traders, proprietors and the like, live closer to Main Street in walled-in concrete houses with SUVs in their driveways and spittoons in their drawing rooms. Pastor Joseph, who used to be the most important person in Fountainville until my mistress, Begum, set up operations, lives on the highest point of town where the Baptist church stands in all its yellow and green glory.

The Baptists, we were taught in school, came and saved us at some point early last century. How they left their country and found us through the Borderlands and the treacherous forests that surround these hills, no one can say for sure, but it is they who are credited with civilising us and abolishing our headhunting ways. Some old-timers say that the coming of the church emasculated our men and drove them into opium dens because they no longer had anything to protect. I say it would have happened anyway.

There are two signposts at the entrance of Fountainville – a weathered stone on the side of the road, which says:

**AFTER WHISKY
DRIVING RISKY**

And the more official, bright-blue hoarding with a few letters smudged away:

*Welcome to Fountainville
Established 1501
Home to world-famous Fountainville Clinic
Please   D   I   E   Slowly*

The fountain, which gives this town its name, lies under the shadow of a giant alder tree. It is an old, dark, magnificent tree whose branches hold thousands of coloured ribbons and cloths – prayer flags – left by the many who have made pilgrimage here. Our women worshipped the fountain for centuries, tended the gardens, made offerings and prayers to placate the spirits. Even when the Baptists came and preached that God was not sun or wind or fire or thunder, they continued to protect the fountain because they understood its magic, how it connected the sky to the earth. 'Keep the fountain safe,' our elders told us, 'and it will keep you safe.' Of course, it did much more than that. It made my mistress famous, and our town something of a visitor attraction.

My mistress is known to everyone as Begum. She is the Lady of the Fountain, and I, Luna, her assistant. It was Begum who discovered the fountain's deeper secrets and entrusted it to our women. She drew them out of fields where they broke their backs threshing corn and drying rice, from sweatshops where they ruined their eyes and fingers embroidering gold threads on pillow cushions so that fat ladies in foreign lands could lie against them. At first she only enlisted the women in our town, but when they heard about the magic, they came from across the mountains and from the seaside too – tall and barrel-shaped, sinister and kind, munificent and stupid. For a while you could meet all kinds of women in Fountainville, and Begum accepted them all.

Of course, there were complaints. Mainly from men who thought it was unnatural, who couldn't bear doing without their wives for months at a time. When their women returned with money in their pockets – money that would've taken them ten years to make, they beat them and called them whores, gambled and drank the money away, then said, 'Maybe you could do it again.' These women would come and go, swelling up with pride and shame, confused about what was right and wrong until their bodies were too used up to do anything.

Whatever complaints anyone might have had

about the fountain, they knew not to complain too loudly because the fountain was the source of our town's changing fortunes, and all those who came into contact with it benefited from its richness. And you and I know that most everyone, whether man or woman or in-between, is crazy for richness.

II

I was born in Fountainville in 1984 and, like most babies at the time, was delivered on the floor of my grandparents' house rather than in the hospital. We didn't trust doctors around here then. They were usually Mainlanders, sent out on two-year missions, thinking they were equipped to handle life in the Borderlands. Most of them struggled with the isolation; the few that didn't capitulate to opium took up a local wife and managed to fool themselves into thinking that this was a life that was always calling for them. I can't think of one happy story that ever transpired between a woman of this town and an outsider, but that's bound to change, the way all things are.

Fountainville is different now. We have running

water, twenty-four hour electricity, doctors and nurses in neat white coats and hairnets and, unless it's animal in nature, no birthing is done on the floor. Funny the way change swoops down so suddenly you can scarcely say how things were before. Used to be that expecting mothers drank at the fountain every day at dusk. Now they just make a prayer before each trimester, tie a little ribbon around the branch of the alder tree and go back to their lives. Rituals have a habit of losing potency too, I suppose, same as anything else.

Our fountain isn't really a fountain, it has to be said. Fountain is just a prettier way of saying *Well* – with a marble slab over it. It's grand enough, being that the marble's over five hundred years old, and the silver cup we use to draw water from the well hasn't tarnished a bit. But it's nothing like the other famous fountains of the world that shoot up high in the air or make music or change colours.

Begum says that the natural underground springs that feed the well are rich in nutrients, which is why avocado and coffee, things that normally do better in warmer climates, thrive so well in our grove. And there's a reason why our women live long, and continue to be so fertile. Every one of us drinks at the fountain at least a couple of times a year. As far as scientific proof goes – well, there isn't any. But belief's a powerful thing, which is why when Begum set up operations she incorporated the fountain as a central part of the process. 'Everyone likes to believe in something outside the limitations of their own bodies,' Begum always said. 'Here, at Fountainville, we can offer that miracle.'

How I came to be Begum's assistant is a strange story. I hardly ever feel the need to unburden myself on others, but not so long ago I found myself doing exactly that with a potential client on Begum's porch. It happened in April, on the day after a crazy hailstorm, which had blown every single leaf off the alder tree. All night the storm raged. It was the most terrifying thing. People hid under beds and in disused bunkers. Two youngsters walking home late got caught in it and were killed. I was in the office, wrapped in blankets at the window. I couldn't sleep.

I watched the sky fill up with lightning – all that noise and fury, and then, stillness. At daybreak, a flock of babblers descended on the bare branches of the alder tree and started singing like a watch of nightingales. Their sound was so miraculous and pure, calling from some place else, refiguring all the broken pieces of the freshly destroyed world. And it was the birds I think, that set me on my own babbling, later, to the stranger on Begum's porch.

'Things always so dramatic around here?' he asked, surveying the grove.

The stranger introduced himself in that stiffly elegant way some foreigners do – with a handshake. I prefer the ones who kiss or leap into immediate intimacy with a bear hug. But the formality of this one suited his appearance. He looked like he'd been lifted straight out of one of those westerns we used to watch when television first came to Fountainville. A town sheriff character in a three-piece suit with immaculate leather boots and an equally immaculate moustache. There was a bit of swagger about him even though he had large, soft, pampered hands that had clearly never saddled a horse or loaded a gun. But the most striking thing about him was the unusual colour of his eyes – a deep sapphire blue, whose magnificence was only somewhat diminished by a pair of rimless spectacles.

'Mind if I smoke?' he asked, before giving his trousers a little tug and sitting down on the steps.

'I had a time of it at the Sanity Boarding House last night,' he said. 'Can you tell me, is that name meant to reassure guests or terrify them?'

'I'm not sure even old Quintus knows why he chose that name,' I said, going in to fetch the registration forms.

The garden was a mess – clusters of strangled leaves everywhere, puddles and mud, bits of broken fence lying about. In the distance I could see that the rainwater harvest pipe on top of the greenhouse had collapsed. I'd need to get the ladder later and fix it back.

'It's going to be fine. Just fine here, I think,' he said, taking the forms. 'My name is Owain, by the way. Owain Knight.'

I liked him immediately. The way he spoke – softly, almost beseechingly, but with authority. The cut of his bespoke suit. His hair, which was dark and kept cropped to stave off the onslaught of curls. But it wasn't sexual, if that's what you're thinking. People always jump to that conclusion as though it couldn't be possible for two strangers to feel immediate kinship. I liked that he carried none of the usual traveller's woes. For someone who had arrived just the day before – into the eye of the storm, so to speak, he was determined to settle in fearlessly.

We sat for a while listening to the babblers, contemplating the greenhouse in the distance. After the storm it looked like one of those cottages you eventually stumble upon in the woods of a childhood fairytale.

'Tell me the strangest story you know,' he said.

And I did.

*

My father was a hardworking man. He farmed, kept

pigs, tutored mathematics, and still had time to give my mother seven children. I was the youngest — the only girl — which meant that I spent most of my childhood running around in my brothers' hand-me-downs. We were poor, so the occasion for a new frock or a beaded necklace happened only once a year, if that, and I'm ashamed to say I coveted those things, yearned for a drawer full of pretty, clean treasures of my own.

My parents met at a harvest dance on a full moon night. My mother was there with her sweetheart, Mr Philo — an arrogant, rodent-looking fellow (as described by my father) who owned a general store and a fancy goods shop on Main Street. 'He had his paws so tight around your mother she couldn't scurry away from him, but she found a way...' My father always teased my mother about her infidelity. 'If only you'd stayed with the rodent, Tania,' he'd say, 'What a different life you could have had.'

They exchanged looks under the glare of the full moon, and every day afterwards, my father followed her home from school, giving her gifts of passion fruit and mango. Apparently, in those days, an exotic fruit was enough to seal the deal. My mother succumbed quickly to my father's persistence and charm, but continued to appear in public with the rodent because she lacked the courage to let him down. When she got pregnant with my eldest brother, she finally ended it by walking into the Philo General Store and announcing to everyone present (his parents were in the background stacking cans) that she was leaving him to marry Vincent Anto. It was my mother's last act of fiery resolve.

They were married at the church shortly after, aged 16 and 17. People thought nothing at the time, of a bride already three months pregnant. It had been the way before, for a couple to test each other out prior to submitting to matrimonial contract. Things are entirely more puritanical these days, but in my parents' time it didn't matter how loudly the Baptists preached against the word fornication. People continued to fornicate behind bushes, in fields and against gravestones in the cemetery, ready to risk hell and brimstone in the hereafter.

My parents were so good at it they produced a band of brothers at the rate of one a year, all named after my father's heroes: Newton, Carl, Euclid, Archimedes (Archie), Jules, and Ramanujan (Ram). I followed respectfully three years later – a sign from somewhere that perhaps they should stop.

I did not care much about my brothers, nor were they very concerned about me. What mattered to them was food. What mattered to me was beauty. I was a bony, nondescript thing with stringy hair and a watered-down version of my father and mother's very weakest genes, as far as looks went. Smarts-wise, I think my father was proud of me. All his sons, with the exception of Newton, had the combined mathematical genius of a gnat. If you'd asked me then, I would have swopped my brains for looks, no questions. But that remained one of those unresolved dreams like the drawer of treasures.

It was not an unhappy childhood, although when I think back to it, all I can remember is waiting for it to be over. I relied greatly upon my imaginative powers for escape and everything might have been different if I'd had a quiet space of my own. But we shared our house with cats and roosters and giant cockroaches, and my father's hogs in the backyard.

We lived in my father's parents' house, which basically consisted of one large, cold room, with the kitchen fire in one corner and the television in the other. This is the room we lived, slept and ate in. All of us: my parents, grandparents, brothers, and me. Only my father's brother, Uncle Manny, had the luxury of his own room – a tumbledown wooden shed erected against the main house. He was an opium addict, and, rather than consigning him to the dens, my grandmother allowed him to live with us, as long as he nursed his addictions in private. My father was keen to send him away because he worried about the influence on his boys. In fact, watching Uncle Manny slowly die, was what kept my brothers off the drugs.

My mother's best friend, Begum, lived next door, and I can't say when exactly the feelings I had for her began to supersede those I had for my mother, but by the time I'd had my first menstruation at twelve, I'd already turned into something horrible with regards to my mother. She had been unable to guide me from childhood into the adult world, worn down from so much mothering and cleaning, I suppose, or perhaps because she was so stuck in her own life she was hardly in a position to advise me. She was always sending me over to Begum's. *Go borrow a cup of lentils, take this leg of lamb over, ask if she has any turnips in the garden…*

I saw Begum as a success in every instance where my mother had failed. Begum had remained youthful. She had married a powerful man called Kedar – a dark, rangy fellow known for smuggling and pimping, but slavish to Begum's every need. They'd had the sense not to have children, so their house resembled more closely what I thought a house should look like – not a battlefield of soiled clothes and pots, but a vast realm of comfort and order with demarcated spaces for privacy and bedrooms with doors. Besides, Begum was the Lady of the Fountain, as her mother had been before. She had incalculable powers. In her house there were shelves of ointments and oils, unguents and potions, all carefully stocked and labelled, ready at hand for any calamity. *Want to make your hair thicker – here – walnut oil and rose petals. Want to soften the force of those migraines – take this.* She was generous in ways my mother couldn't be. And she was beautiful. 'Promise me,' I used to say, 'If you ever go away from here, you'll take me with you.'

Begum had an idea to go to the Mainland to learn about starting a business. 'No one sees very far in this town, Luna,' she was always saying, 'They can't see beyond their weekly wage and drink. I'm going to change all that.'

When my brother Newton graduated from university (he was the first person in our family to study in the Mainland), my father decided we should all get on a bus and go to the Mainland for a week. I'd never seen my father looking so proud, standing a few inches taller, walking around with his hands in his pockets, telling everyone that his Newton was going to be an engineer. I had been promised a new dress and a trip to the zoo to see tigers and zebras and animals I'd only ever seen on television. All my life I'd wanted to leave Fountainville, so I was almost as surprised as everyone else when I pulled my father aside and told him I wouldn't be going with them. 'I just can't do it,' I said, 'Don't ask me to explain, I just can't.'

Begum later said it was a visitation. My father walked me over there, standing at the threshold to her house with his hat in his hands. 'This child's too stubborn for me, Begum,' he said. He looked so old then – my hardworking father, like a small, bent tree at the top of a cliff.

'Here,' he said, slipping his wedding ring off his finger and putting it in my palms, 'Keep this safe for me.'

He fussed with his spectacles that he'd been talked into getting very recently, sliding them further up his nose. And then he touched my shoulder before turning to join my mother and brothers, who were standing around a pile of bags.

That was my last image of them.

A week later, when the men tried to pull what was left of the bus from the mountainside, they would not find the bodies of my family or any of the others who had been travelling back from the Mainland.

A farmer, who had been bringing his cows home from pasture, was the only witness to what happened. 'One minute I saw a bus moving along the hillside,' he said, 'the next, it was gone, just like that.'

After the accident I learned to become invisible. I moved into Begum's house while the town elders decided what should happen with my parents' property and possessions. Begum said I had special gifts. She said God had perhaps had a plan when he didn't give her any children of her own.

III

I was taught how to become invisible by Rafi, the keeper of the forest. Rafi lived alone in a hut at the periphery of the Northern Forest Ridge, past the terraced farmlands and brick houses, out past the thickets of mahogany and timber, into the deeper forest where leopards and bears and drug-traffickers roamed.

Rafi was the ugliest man you ever saw – seven feet tall with one good leg and one gimpy leg, one good eye and one cloudy. No one knew where he came from or who his parents were. We all assumed he'd run away from the circus. Once a week he would come to Main Street to buy a litre of whisky from Xerxes, the bootlegger. You'd think he was a kind man, the way the animals followed him – dogs, cats, horses, cows – when they saw him, they followed, as if he were the Pied Piper. Except Rafi didn't play a pipe, and he wasn't leading them anywhere.

A few weeks after I lost my family I saw Rafi sitting on the stoop of the Glory Hallelujah teahouse, rolling a smoke with those giant fingers of his. It was a magical autumn day, the sky so blue and clear, it made you forget you were in Fountainville. Forget about the gutters overflowing with garbage, and those silly housewives squatting on their haunches selling bits of turd-like vegetables dug up from their gardens. Trees were beginning to sport little skirts of red foliage around their waists and lichens at their feet, and everything everywhere was festooned in a glorious coppery light.

It made you want to believe in something. At least, that's what I was thinking, when I heard: THWACK THWACK THWACK.

Rafi had made paddles of his fists and, for some reason I couldn't immediately fathom, was swinging them sideways into the heads of three dogs. These weren't Pomeranians, mind, they were sly, unforgiving hill mongrels who in a pack, could tear a person to bits. They were sitting at his feet like lambs, taking it: THWACK THWACK THWACK.

'You,' Rafi said, when he caught me staring, 'What are you looking at?'

'You should be happy you don't live in a civilised place,' I shouted, 'Someone could report you to the SPCA.'

He snorted, mimicking me. 'ES PEE SEE EY!'

'That's right. Those dogs aren't doing anything to bother you. Why the hell are you smacking them in the head like that?'

'Darling,' he said, 'if I treated you as kind as I treat these dogs, you'd think you'd died and gone to heaven.'

At which point, I started bawling. Crying from the very bottom of my toes. It was a deluge – salt, snot, bodily fluids of which I didn't know the names – dripping out of my eyes and nose and mouth. Twitching, blubbering, crazy-kind of crying.

Since the accident I hadn't been able to cry, no matter how hard Begum and Kedar tried to get it out of me. Not alone in bed at night, not during my walks, not in the many corners of my new house where I'd found my much-desired loneliness.

I had hoped to be traumatised by ghosts – eleven of them. To hear my father's footsteps following me, trying to catch me and ask, *How could you save yourself, Luna, and not the others?* My mother, thrashing around in Begum's kitchen like a hurricane, saying, *Happy? Happy you're with your beloved Begum now that you killed us, you little bitch.* But no such luck. It was dead-deadening-deadest silence. The spirits of my family were either lost or did not think me worth haunting.

The truth is I hadn't had any inkling or prophecy, no matter what anyone believed. The reason I hadn't gone to Newton's graduation ceremony with the rest of my family was because I was ashamed. Isn't a fourteen year old allowed to be unreasonable about her indignities? I didn't want to travel in that beat-up bus with our beat-up peasant clothes and beat-up suitcases, to arrive in the Mainland only to be told: *Hey Chinky, why don't you make us some chop-suey?*

Newton had written about his difficulties in his letters home. He hadn't held a thing back – all the dirty things those Mainlanders called him – his landlady, the taxi drivers, even some of the professors, who were so surprised about his mathematical abilities. Poor Newton survived all that, survived growing up in Fountainville and getting out, only to die falling down a hillside.

'Hey, hey!' Rafi said, reaching his big arm toward me. 'Settle it down. Is this about the dogs, or something else?'

'Both.'

'Well, you better tell me about that something else then.'

And so I began, as I too often do: telling my deepest secrets to a stranger.

★

'Walk with me,' Rafi said, after I told him the whole story. 'I want to show you something.'

He led me all the way to the church, dragging his

40

gimpy leg slowly up the hill. Those three dogs, dizzy-headed no doubt, followed us like a patrol.

'Tell me what you see,' he said, pointing to what lay below.

'I see Main Street and I see the tops of trees and a few billboards, and I see people coming out of the cinema, and I see Pastor Joseph snoozing in his chair.'

'That's what I thought,' he said, 'You don't see much, do you?

'You know why I hit those dogs?' he added, curling his fists into paddles again. 'I got love in one hand, and punishment in the other, because that's the code of the universe. Fear and love. They go together.'

'That's ridiculous,' I interrupted. 'What about St Francis of Assisi? He didn't go around walloping harmless creatures on the head.'

'Francis of Assisi! You are a funny one. Do I look like a fucking saint to you?

'Listen, girl, you know what your gift is? Not that you can divine the future, not that you can curse your enemies, none of that, because the truth is no one can do that. Your greatest gift is that you are utterly forgettable. If you learn to shut your trap, that is.

'Do you think people look at you when you walk down the street? Sorry to break your heart, darling, but no, they don't. You might as well be a cement wall. Do you think they look at me though? Oh, they do. They fix their wicked eyes upon me and think nothing of letting their gaze stay there, staring and staring. Do you think they wonder, *How the hell did he get like that? Lame in one leg and blind in one eye and keeling over like a leaning tower.* They do. That and worse. But you – piddling, nondescript girl. You're lucky. You could go anywhere, see anything, and no one would even notice.

'What you have is freedom. Hold on to it. And learn to use your goddamn eyes.'

He left me up there on the hill. 'I'll be seeing you, missy,' he said, waving a balled-up fist in the air jovially, while the dogs trotted behind him.

I turned and walked back to the top of Main Street. I stood on the corner and stared at people passing by, hoping to catch someone's eye. Not a chance. Their glances went above my head and across my shoulder and right through my belly. It was as if I wasn't even there.

I walked west – across into the forbidden zone of dens and brothels and saloons. I was terrified. As children we had been warned off this part of town by our parents. Later, as an adult, I didn't need anyone to tell me that only a certain kind of woman ventured here. Everything seemed meaner, dirtier, without the slightest hope of redemption.

There were things I'd never seen before: whores standing on balconies with their tits hanging out and half-dead men sucking on pipes. Beggars with stumps for arms and blackened buildings rotting in the howling sun. There was a smell of death that hung heavy and threatening, clinging to all the ramshackle buildings and souls that inhabited them. I walked and walked through it all waiting for someone to say, *What's a girl like you doing in a place like this? Don't you know it's dangerous?*

But no one saw, no one spoke. Rafi was right. My face was my fortune.

IV

When Begum was a young girl she was so beautiful she was kidnapped by a drug-lord and forced to live in his jungle hideout for three weeks. His name was Haroon Sheriff, and he was one of the meanest men who ever inhabited the pages of Fountainville's history. Long after he was killed, parents still warned their children about the dangers of talking to strangers. 'Haroon Sheriff has ears and eyes everywhere,' they said. 'If you're not careful he's going to get you.'

On the summer solstice of 1978, Haroon Sheriff sent three of his men to wait for Begum by the school gates. Begum was fourteen. She had thick black hair, which lay plaited like two coiled snakes on either side of her head, breasts like torpedoes, and skin as soft as a Chinese whisper. When she spoke people listened, not so much for what she was saying, but for the way her lips formed two pink cushions around the words she uttered. At least, this is how Kedar tells it; he was 18 at the time, and the head of a very long line of Begum's admirers.

Begum's father was an important man in the town council. He was a greedy, unintelligent man with a fondness for fried food, so it was easy for Sheriff's men to dress in police uniforms and fool her – tell her that her father had suffered a heart attack; that she must hurry-hurry with them. Begum – distraught, followed them into their jeep. When they drove past the hospital, out past the forest ridge and into the deeper jungle, she knew the worst was waiting for her.

Soon after I went to live with Begum and Kedar she told me all about it. 'I thought they were going to rape me, strangle me, leave my body out for the wolves. Do you know what they did instead, Luna? They prepared a bed for me with soft, cotton sheets; gave me a bucket of water to wash with; laid out a dress of blue and gold.

'At six in the evening one of his men knocked and asked if I was ready. He led me blindfolded through a winding tunnel and after a while – I can't say how long, I was made to sit and wait for Haroon Sheriff.

'He was an ordinary man, Luna. I mean, he could have been anyone. When my blindfold was removed, I looked across the table, which was laid with fine plates and cutlery, dishes of rice and meat, mountains of fruit – and there, in front of me, was the most feared man of Fountainville. I couldn't believe it. There was nothing to him – medium height, medium build, medium everything. The only noticeable thing about him was a small birthmark on his left cheek in the shape of a seashell. I'd expected an ogre. Instead – this man, with his neat hair and freshly shaven face, speaking in the most perfectly modulated voice. 'My dear,' he said, 'I'm sorry for what you had to go through. I hope you managed to rest a bit.'

'He was completely insane, of course. Cuckoo! In his mind he was saving me from the wickedness of the world. He spoke of his love for me as something pure, undiluted. He would not test that love until I was ready. He did not touch me, Luna. In all the twenty-one days and nights I stayed in that jungle with him, he did not touch me. The only thing he asked for, and which I permitted, was for him to lay his head down in my lap to weep. He was such a sad man, filled with so much guilt and madness. Every night, after dinner, his men would leave the room, and Haroon Sheriff, Fountainville's most dreaded dacoit, soaked my skirt with his tears. And I, in my weakest moments, stroked his head and forgave him.

'If I hadn't been rescued, who knows what might have happened? I might have even fallen in love with him. You read about it all the time in the papers – those horrors who keep little girls locked up in their basements, children who are treated worse than cattle and never allowed in the sun. And because they don't know any better, or because you love the hand that feeds you even if it kills you, they begin to feel something like tenderness towards their captors. And I can understand why. Everything changes in those circumstances – what's natural, what's not.

Something like gratitude begins to develop; the idea that you no longer have to worry about the world. All that is important is that someone is protecting you, feeding you, clothing you. Things fall away. It's a strange kind of existence with no real markers of time. Days upon days. Nights upon nights.

'Sometimes his men kept me blindfolded even when I was in my room, just so I wouldn't be able to read magazines or paint pictures. I'd close my eyes and think about my lessons from school, which made little sense in that place. I'd think about my parents, my friends, but after a while even they faded into a dream world, and I was unsure whether it was I who was lost, or they. It could have gone on like that for a very long time. I never made any attempt to run because I knew it was useless. His goons would have caught me and taken away the few freedoms I was allowed.

'I didn't expect to be saved. We were so deep in the jungle, and no one had seen me leave. The hide-out was surrounded by a thicket of trees. There were secret underground tunnels, vaults and pits – all reeking of bats. That final night, at dinner, I thought a bomb had dropped down on us from the sky. We were eating, and I still remember the taste of that country chicken on my tongue, when there was a scuffling sound, and a loud shot. Haroon's head bounced backwards, then forwards again. His entire body flopped neatly into the dishes on the table, darkening the wood with his blood. I must have fainted, because when I opened my eyes, all I saw was Kedar standing in front of me with a shotgun in his hand. He had killed Haroon Sheriff with a single bullet to the head. And that was it for me. Love at first sight. Finished.'

★

The rescuing of Begum from the hideout of Haroon Sheriff, and the decimation of his men by Kedar and his gang, is a story that has acquired mythic proportions in this town. Whenever I hear it or tell it, new embellishments get added. Haroon Sheriff's birthmark becomes a stain that covers his entire cheek; at the moment of his death he transforms into a raven and flies off into the woods; Kedar is supposed to have discovered Sheriff's hideout with the help of a band of forest monkeys. But all this is speculation. What's true is what I've just told you. Nothing more, nothing less. And that's why Begum changed her life.

Begum was a big believer in fate. 'My destiny waited for me, Luna,' she told me. 'My destiny was the greenhouse, and it waited for me to discover that there was something bigger than Kedar, or the fountain, or this town – something I had to find myself. When I think about that blindfold placed over my eyes when I was fourteen, I often think it's the first time I actually learned to see. You know the role of blindness in our folk tales, Luna? Only in darkness can you begin to see light. After Kedar rescued me I started to think about new ways of seeing. For so many years I caught glimpses of what my destiny could be. I'd see it, as you see the dawn, through bleary eyes – almost catching it, but then succumbing to sleep, only to wake and find you're no closer to it than you ever were. The only thing I desired in life was to discover that thing which would remove the blindfold forever. And it happened just as I thought it would – like a thunderclap; a single shot going off in the forest. The day I had the idea for the greenhouse – that moment, everything lifted. I could see clear and far ahead. My life's purpose was no longer a mystery.'

*

There's a photo of Begum and Kedar on their wedding day. He's wearing a dark suit looking rather seriously at the camera – hair flattened evenly on both sides of his parting, smile in check. Begum looks dishevelled, not her most beautiful. Her wedding dress has fallen off one shoulder, exposing a mound of smooth round flesh. There's confetti in her dark tousled hair. She looks as if she's been running at a terrific speed because her cheeks are red, and the way she gazes at Kedar is already tinged with a kind of exhausted devotion. I wonder what she's thinking in that photograph: how much in love she is, or how much longer it's possible to love like this, or is this the real beginning of her life? It's an iconic picture, capturing their truest selves – all their insecurities and triumphs. Nothing like my parent's wedding photograph which seems a falsity; two imposters dragged in to act the role. They're standing on the steps of the church with their arms interlocked as if they're set to go off on a voyage. Childlessness suits them. Light, formless, young. I want to tell them – *Wait, stay here in this moment, make it last a little longer!* But their eyes are unafraid of the future. They're looking at it with all the intensity and fervour that only the very young and innocent can have, believing everything will be well, that they will come through unscathed.

V

We keep twenty-four women in the greenhouse at a time. Each gets a bed, a side-table, linen and socks for the duration of their stay. The beds are lined up twelve on each side, and a mirror hangs on the south wall, just big enough for them to see their faces. Most women bring pictures of their family to stick above their beds. Some bring small statues of gods, crosses or lucky charms, which they lodge in the windowsill. In the adjacent common room there's a flat-screen TV, which alternates between soap operas and news channels. All the women congregate here day and night, staring dumbly at the box like a row of watermelons, instead of working on Sudoku or embroidery – activities we recommend.

The only mandatory daily activities are the

morning meditation session, which Begum leads, and the evening drink at the fountain. We suggest half an hour of gentle daily exercise – just a stroll in the garden or a slow meander around the lily pond, but it's impossible to enforce this. We also offer computer lessons, but very few actually make use of them. They're bored of course, and everything is strange to them – the environment, the changes they must undergo, their own bodies. Some of them are so young, often away from their families for the first time. So they mope about, forever texting their husbands about the hardship of it all.

Every one of them calculates what they will do with the money before they've got it. This is inevitable I suppose, but Begum and I try to foster a sense of sisterhood in the greenhouse, the idea that they're working towards a greater good, and that money should not be their only motivation.

Communal living has its pitfalls, the worst being that people divide quickly into cliques. In the past we've had to deal with everything from petty arguments about who stole who's soap to full-scale battles about personal honour. And given the rotating nature of the women we hire as proxies, we never know when problems will erupt. With all proxies, even those who are illiterate (and there's a fair number of them), we make sure to cover the basics before they get here so they're as prepared as they can possibly be.

★

FOUNTAINVILLE CLINIC GUIDELINES FOR PROXIES

1. All proxies must drink at the fountain once daily at 6pm.
2. Please pack comfortable clothing and bring something warm as evenings can get cool. There will be no occasion for dressing up.
3. Do not bring jewellery, watches or any items of value.
4. Do bring items that can help pass time: knitting, embroidery etc.
5. All personal items must fit into trunk under bed (3.5ft high, 4ft width).
6. Family members and guests are NOT allowed to visit.

7. TV, library, board games, playing cards, and all hygiene products will be provided.
8. Meals will be served thrice a day in the dining room. Breakfast 8am, Lunch 1pm, Dinner 7pm. Fruit and healthy snacks will be available all day. No outside food allowed.
9. Gambling, smoking, drinking and unauthorised drugs will not be tolerated.
10. No one may leave the compound under any circumstances without contacting Luna or Begum.
11. Any proxy found engaging in ganging up on, or bullying another proxy will be forced to terminate the contract and prevented from further engagement with the clinic.
12. No proxies are allowed to instigate personal relationships with clients. Anyone found breaching this code will be blacklisted and all contractual agreements will be nullified.

★

Our first proxy was a woman called Asmara, wife of the farmer Binoy Louis. She was built like a house with large flat hands and legs overrun by varicose veins. 'Surely she's too old?' Begum whispered when Asmara walked in the front door.

'I hear you pay five thousand,' Asmara said. 'I'll take half that.'

Asmara was our beginning. A fearless, fat housewife who had clearly reached the ditch-water of her troubles. She didn't complain once about having to spread her legs; about the injections or blood tests or probes. She just closed her eyes and relented like a patient cow. Because she was our first, and for a while, our only proxy, she told us everything. That her husband Binoy had worked his fields from four in the morning to six in the evening every day for fifteen years and *still* didn't have a good shirt to show for church. That she was in love with a movie star and when her husband made love to her (which was rare these days), she asked him to flip her over like an omelette so she could better imagine the movie star. That she sometimes hated her children, God help her, but they were an ungrateful bunch of wretches. Only the middle one, her second son, gave her hope. He studied all night with the help of a torchlight and dissected frogs in school. Soon they would have to buy him a thick pair of spectacles and other boys would bully him, but what an intelligent fellow he was going to be.

'How tiring it is to be poor,' Asmara once told me, and in the very next breath, 'So when are you going to have children, Luna? Or at least, find a man?'

I could only laugh. 'Do I look like a sheep to you?' I said. 'When I open my mouth do you hear me say baa? Why do you think, especially when you tell me stories like this, that I'm dying to go out and do what every foolish woman in this town has done?'

Asmara understood. She said I was right, of course, to take my freedom seriously. 'But don't become a bitter old woman, Luna. Make room for love, otherwise life can be so long.'

When Asmara finished her three stints at the clinic, Dr Willis put her on medication, after having ascertained that an underactive thyroid was the reason for her fatness. Overnight, Asmara shrank to half her size. Features that had been hiding for decades resurfaced like rosebuds. There was nothing to do about the flat hands and big potato nose but, thinned out, Asmara looked quite different. After all those years of carrying extra weight, it emerged that Asmara had a waist, which gave her body a certain elegance, and allowed her to move about with renewed litheness. All the women in town thought we were conducting age-defying experiments at the clinic.

'How many fatties do you think have asked where they can sign up?' grinned Asmara, when she came to visit. 'I'll be asking for my ten percent finder's fee.'

Proxies who came after Asmara tried to foist their life stories upon me but I made it clear from the beginning that it wouldn't increase our chances of friendship. It was not out of apathy that I did this, but for my own self-preservation. I knew that I would then be expected to return the favour and share my life stories with them, but that privilege was reserved for strange men who drifted into my life, like Rafi or Mr Knight.

★

I remember clearly when Mr Knight showed up on Begum's porch that April day after the storm. He walked so quickly into the centre of my life, it's difficult to think of a time when we didn't know each other. The reason he came to Fountainville was because of Asmara. His friends back home, Cei and Cynon – our first gentlemen clients – had told him that if ever there was a woman to change your life, it was Asmara. Somehow it wasn't difficult for me to imagine them all – Mr Cynon, Mr Cei and Mr Knight, sitting around a table in some foreign country where everything was cleaner, richer, more beautiful. A long table filled with food and drink, music playing in the background, and women with hair like golden trumpets sitting beside them.

Of course, it would be impossible to engage Asmara as she'd completed her time at the clinic, but I told Mr Knight we could find someone else. 'And how are Mr Cynon and Cei doing?' I asked.

'Elated,' he said. 'Beyond elated. They tell me I can't see the forest from the trees. To hear them describe it, nothing could be more geared to a man's needs than this clinic of yours. They've mythologised it you see – everything is glowing, beautiful, bright, fantastic. But I have my reservations. In the end I just had to come see for myself.'

'Indecision is never a good thing.'

'It's just not as simple as I think they'd like it to be. I mean there are basic things that still haven't been thought through, and no one has any idea what the psychological impact is going to be on us all ten, twenty years down the line... it seems unnatural, somehow.'

'Lots of things seem unnatural when they start out, but that doesn't mean they're not right. I don't mean to try and persuade you in one direction or the other, but obviously I'm biased.'

As we walked up the path towards the greenhouse, Sabina – the self-appointed leader of our current group of proxies, walked out of the bath house in a nightgown and a towel on her head. I do not like

Sabina — not because she's pretty, but because she's educated, and she lords her literacy over the other proxies instead of helping them. She comes from the neighbouring town of Somaville, from a chieftain family fallen on hard times. She arrived alone, as most of these women do, with no family or friend to escort her.

'New client?' she said, pausing to stare at Mr Knight.

'Mr Knight is thinking of working with Chanu Rose,' I said, even though I had no idea if Mr Knight even wanted to work with us.

'Oh, Chanu Rose! That's nice. Good luck, Mr Knight,' Sabina said, walking away, her hips careening from side to side like a pendulum.

I noticed Mr Knight didn't watch Sabina like other men did, which was understandable, proper. Everything about him was so neat and precise and continually pleasing to me.

'Don't be afraid, Mr Knight,' I said, as we approached the door to the greenhouse. 'Are you ready for your future?'

VI

A month after Mr Knight arrived in Fountainville a woman claiming to be Sabina's sister showed up at the gates of the clinic. She was skinny and loud, and any beauty she might once have possessed had been sucked out of her by the pipe. She wanted money, she said. Their father was gambling, her child needed medicines.

'You up and leave and now I have to be the bloody nurse,' she screeched, hanging on to the gate like a banshee.

Rule six clearly prohibited family members from visiting, although Begum was known to relent in special cases. With Mr Knight, for instance, she had simply thrown out Rule 12.

'He's nice to have around,' she said. 'A little bit of

testosterone can't harm.'

And it was true. If we'd known that the presence of a man could rouse the proxies from their walrus-like state of indolence, we might have relaxed the no-male staff rule earlier. Most men of course, were not Mr Knight. They could always be relied upon to grope or inappropriately fondle a proxy regardless of the state she was in. As it was, cleavage that had been tucked away suddenly popped out on display. Rivalries between proxy groups were soothed with the trade of a few tubes of lipstick, and demands for a parlour girl to come in to thread eyebrows were universal.

'You told us we wouldn't need to dress up,' the proxies complained. 'We feel like dishrags when Mr Knight see us like this – lounging around in our nighties all day.'

Mr Knight had befriended all the proxies systematically, coaxing their histories out of them while giving very little of himself away. He was softest on Chanu Rose. He'd found out that no one in her family knew she was here except for her sister.

Chanu had lied to her husband and told him she was going to the Mainland to get a degree in secretarial studies. If he found out what she was really doing he would surely kill her. She had a picture of her husband above her bed – a square-jawed, too-pleased-with-himself-looking man with a mean mouth and surprisingly soft, beautiful brown eyes. She cried most nights and none of the proxies comforted her.

For Chanu Rose's twenty-fourth birthday Mr Knight decorated the entire greenhouse with streamers and balloons, and had Mitsy, the head cook, march in with a big chocolate cake singing Happy Birthday. I don't think anyone had ever done anything like that for her before. She was bawling like a duck, of course. I swear she'd leave her husband if she could – the way she went on about Mr Knight this, Mr Knight that.

Begum was the bigger surprise though. She had become increasingly suspicious of outsiders ever since a damning article had been published in a foreign newspaper attacking the ethics of running a cloistered-style greenhouse such as ours, and accusing Begum of 'antiquated gender politics'. The woman who wrote the article had posed as a potential client and spent a month in Fountainville collecting data. The reporter and Begum had spent several afternoons discussing the great feminists of the world, and Begum had been made to believe she was one of them. The betrayal had been devastating.

Given that Mr Knight still hadn't declared his intentions, Begum was being remarkably open with him. They played chess in her office between appointments − a single game often lasting an entire week. Begum, always a sore loser, was almost as unbearable when she won. 'Think harder, Mr Knight,' she'd say, jabbing her finger in the air when she finally checkmated him. 'You're playing with a master.'

In reality, he had been the real master, slowly gaining her confidence by helping to reorganise the filing system at the clinic, and by giving her ideas to expand her business. When he discovered that she had a room full of jars and unguents to suit every kind of ailment in the world, and that these recipes had been handed down from one Lady of the Fountain to the next, and that all the ingredients were handpicked from the local forests, he immediately set about branding, designing and packaging La Saĝon de Fountainville – a health and beauty line to be sold in the finest boutiques.

Mr Knight was a taxonomist by profession, which he explained, had nothing to do with collecting taxes. He was a kind of biologist, whose job it was to make order of things – classifying species, naming them, putting them in hierarchy. I doubted it was his real job, or the job that sustained his lifestyle, as he appeared to be a gentleman of wealthy means, but it explained a good deal about the way he conducted himself, and his compulsive need for order.

'You're sitting on a gold mine,' he told Begum. 'If we can get this wellness line going you won't need to do anything else. It's exactly the sort of thing self-engrossed, fair-trade liberals like myself are interested in spending money on!'

'Even men?' Begum asked.

'Absolutely. In fact, you could tailor it just for men,

and it would still make you millions.'

I wasn't jealous of their burgeoning friendship, although the same couldn't be said for Kedar, who believed that Mr Knight was another undercover journalist – 'a wolf dressed up as a fluffy sheep'.

In the beginning, there were pangs, I'll admit, but those had more to do with my own reticence than Mr Knight being liberal with his charm. He insisted that I call him by his first name. Impossible, of course. The best I could do was call him Mr Owain.

It was Mr Owain who insisted we bring Sabina's sister inside rather than leave her screaming at the gate. The sisters sat on the garden bench for an hour, talking softly, sometimes touching fingers, until an agreement was reached. A small bundle of notes were prised out from Sabina's blouse and thrust into her sister's hands.

'Well, that's her straight to the den,' I said.

'Will you take me to see those places?' Mr Owain asked. 'I think I need to see them to understand.'

I had already told him about the epidemic that affected our Borderlands – a pandemic, really. Drugs from the opium fields across the mountains came through here before making their way to the chemical labs in the Mainland. Kilos of heroin smuggled over in jute bags. Most of our young people didn't bother with pipes. They shot up wherever they could – in toilets and bunkers, some of them as young as ten, most of them illiterate. They shared needles because they didn't know better, and because they couldn't always get hold of fresh ones. So there wasn't just the problem of addiction but widespread HIV, which the Mainland and our own church refused to acknowledge. I had told him all about my Uncle Manny's slow and sorry death, about a classmate who'd been raped by army men, about truckers and prostitution – basically everything I hated about this town, but he still wanted to see for himself.

'Perhaps I could get involved, do something useful while I'm here being indecisive about other things?'

'Why don't you discuss it with Pastor Joseph?'

'You can't be serious,' he said. 'The man is still

banging on about the sin of premarital sex. He thinks condoms have holes through which the Aids virus can pass. He doesn't even allow the burial of drug addicts. He's worse than the Pope!'

★

We waited till dusk and wrapped ourselves in heavy coats and balaclavas against the cold and the prying eyes. I took him past the cemetery, westward, where the tarred road gave way to a rickety wooden bridge, and on the other side, a narrow pitted mud track strewn with garbage. The houses here were sloping structures built haphazardly on bamboo stilts, leaning precariously over a sludge of river with thin columns of smoke spewing from their chimneys. Even the trees seemed diminished and wasted.

Moving through this part of town always felt to me like descending into the circles of hell – becoming more and more grotesque as you advanced. On the periphery, there were the houses of disrepute – gambling dens and whorehouses – sprinkled along the river's edge so the honourable people could slip across this way and that. Further out were the so-called mad houses, which were really rudimentary homes for the dispossessed – children with disabilities who had been dumped there, the terminally sick, the old, the insane, the tortured and the lost. There were black flags on some of these houses. These were the marks of death: leprosy, cholera, TB, HIV. Still further, towards the dangerous borders at the foothills, and beyond, where the fields of poppies bloomed – were the dens. Desolate places: dark and fragrant all at once. Once you arrived there, it was difficult to make your way back.

'It's like the end of the world,' Mr Owain said, pinching his nose with his fingers.

'You'll get used to it.'

The path was lit by a few street lamps. On a moonlit night you could negotiate your way easily, but we held torches to make sure not to step on one of the many stinking collapsed heaps along the way – animal or human, dead or dying – it was impossible to tell. I took Mr Owain into the oldest den in

Fountainville — a two-storey structure, which was filled mostly with men, lying on their sides like derelicts — on cots and mats, some behind bamboo screens, others in full view, sucking on long bamboo pipes.

'This looks like a scene from a hundred years ago,' he said. 'Really, it's unbelievable.'

There were half-dressed skeletal women moving about filling the pipes. The proprietor — a fat, moustachioed gent, whose eyes had completely disappeared into the folds of his cheeks, sat with a whore on his lap, twitching his chubby fingers in the air for us to come over.

'I have a better room upstairs,' he said. 'This is for the locals.'

'Okay,' Mr Owain said. 'Let's see it.'

'You, Petal, you take them up.'

The whore sprang off the proprietor's meaty thigh and led us to the top room, offering Mr Owain the range of her services along the way, which he politely declined.

'You like them younger?' she asked. 'Girls? Boys?

Tell me. We have it all.'

'Just show us the room,' I said.

She scowled. 'Relax, little sister.'

The upstairs chamber had only five people in it. All of them men – one who vaguely resembled a doctor who'd gone missing a few years ago after a botched abortion. The others could have been Mainlanders who never made their way back. Each of the men had his own bed by the window. The air was less dense up here, the room brighter.

'Their families pay every month,' the whore said. 'We look after them. Give them baths and food. Not that they care about that. We keep them away from the riff-raff. You want to try a pipe, Sir? I'll make you the sweetest pipe you ever had.'

'We should go,' I said, pulling Mr Owain towards the stairway.

'Come back and see me now,' the whore smiled, pinching his bum.

★

Things changed afterwards. Before that excursion Mr Knight used to come to the clinic everyday. He watched soap operas with the proxies and learned to knit little pairs of socks. He played chess and helped the gardener harvest tomatoes. Now he spent more time on the west-side with the sole outreach programme operating in Fountainville. The House of Hope was run by a young couple – Binita and Matthew Samuel, who had both studied Economics and Development in the Mainland, and had returned home to make a difference. They had started a drop-in centre for HIV counselling and had initiated various grassroots campaigns for condom promotion and syringe exchange in the tobacco shops. They were forever organising Christian rock concerts in the hope of trying to get the pastor on their side. Mr Owain was their new shining star in this regard. Their hope was that he would be able to convince Pastor Joseph to use the church as a platform for activism.

I began visiting Mr Owain most evenings at the Sanity Boarding House for tea as this was the time the proxies were busiest with activities that didn't require my attention. Mr Quintus, the owner of the SBH, reserved the corner table on the veranda for us. He threw a faded blue cloth over the table, which lent it an air of dilapidated elegance, and he made sure there was a steady supply of tea, fruit cake and banana fritters from the kitchen. He even allowed Mr Owain to keep his flask of whisky in plain sight, though the SBH wasn't licensed to sell liquor. When I arrived, Mr Owain would be in his corner, scribbling in his notebooks.

'What's so great about Fountainville that you're always writing about it?'

'Everything,' he'd say, beaming. 'I write about what I hear and see, what I think and feel. If I don't write, I forget. It's the strangest place, Luna. Extraordinary. You don't realise it.'

We had long discussions about how to bring change to the Borderlands. He was filled with that messianic do-gooding fervour that I would have found irritating with anyone else. He once made the mistake of saying how people here had so little yet they seemed much happier than anywhere else in the world.

'Don't romanticise things,' I snapped. 'Whatever you do, don't do that. They talk of economic progress in the Mainland, but they don't do anything for us. They want our men to fight in their army, our women to work in their restaurants and factories – cleaning up after them. For what? To be second-class citizens? We didn't have running water here until Begum started this clinic. If Kedar hadn't gone to the Mainland to cut a deal with the Minister of Health and Family Welfare, we'd still be living in the dark ages. If we appear to be happy, it's only because of some misguided idea that we must make do, and eventually there'll be more to life than shit.

'Oh, I feel better now,' I laughed, looking at his startled reaction. 'Better not get me started.'

Some days he seemed so far away I couldn't tell if it was the troubles of Fountainville or something closer to his heart. To live here so many weeks, the only foreigner in town – looking at all the dirty, degrading things that had little chance of improving, it wasn't an easy thing.

'Don't you miss home?' I asked regularly, hoping to find out about a family, a lover, something that might be beckoning.

He admitted that the homesickness crept up from time to time so suddenly he could do nothing but stay in his room all day. 'But if I went back I'd only think about all that I was missing here. It's my limitation. I want to be in two places at once.'

People in town had begun to whisper about us but I didn't care. Sitting with him every evening and watching the sun go down like a forest fire in the sky – those blood-red embers lighting up the thatch roofs of Fountainville, was a daily act of grace I'd come to rely upon.

Mr Owain sometimes reached for my hand across the table, and I'd give it to him, easily. I wouldn't be exaggerating if I said I hadn't felt this returned to the world since I lost my family. It was as if I had a shot at goodness again. We both did.

VII

Begum had the idea for the greenhouse after watching a TV programme. This was five years after I'd been living with her and Kedar. I was nineteen then – still bone-thin and nondescript, despite Begum's many beauty administrations. I remember her coming home one evening after visiting Papa Davy, who had just lost his wife to cancer, and who seemed to be dying of something terrible himself. Begum would go over a couple of times a day to give the old man something for the pain – morphine, usually. Sometimes she'd take me with her, and I'd stand in the corner, watching, while she held his gnarly hand, rubbing cream into his cuticles, cooing nonsense into his ear. Sometimes she just sat by his side in silence while the TV or radio played softly in the background. Begum always knew how to comfort a person.

One day she came home looking like she'd taken a hit of morphine herself. I'd never seen her like that before – eyes all glassy, slurring her words. I took hold of her hand and led her inside the house. Begum, having grown a little hefty in the thighs over the years, lowered herself quickly into a chair, giving her customary pleated maxi skirt a whoosh when she sat down. I brought her a glass of lemon water and asked what the matter was. She kept looking ahead at the open door of the house with this stunned look on her face as if she'd been shot in the stomach. Then she took my hand and squeezed my knuckles hard.

'Luna,' she said, 'It's finally going to happen.'

I couldn't get it out of her, no matter how many glasses of lemon water I plied her with. She kept saying, 'It's here, it's here,' like one of those crazy fundamentalists at church. It took Kedar coming home to make sense of it.

Kedar kept odd hours owing to the irregular

nature of his job. He was what you'd call a fixer – a man in the know with an ear to the town's drug-dealers, hit-men, government officials, elders, pastor and policemen. His services ranged from the quotidian to the grotesque. If, for example, you wanted to start a bakery on Main Street, or a second-hand electronic goods store – Kedar would be the man to get you your license. If your demands were more complicated – say you wanted to take possession of a disputed property, Kedar could point you in the right direction. Needless to say card tables, pimping girls and dope all fell under his sway.

For a gangster Kedar smiled a lot. I used to be terrified of him as a child. He was so perfectly symmetrical – tall and sinewy, with wavy jet-black hair divided in a centre parting, and sideburns that were never allowed to run awry. Long before it became fashionable to sport muscles in Fountainville, Kedar used to stand in the yard in a wrestling singlet, lifting dumb-bells diligently until his biceps popped out like two hillocks. I was fascinated by Kedar's biceps, not just because he massaged oil into them, making them glisten, but for the tattoos sprawled over the entire girth of them — a coiled serpent on the left bicep, and on the right, entwined around the stem of a rose, the letters *B e g u m*.

Kedar had the reputation of being a fair man. While he may have had a pinkie in every dirty dealing around town, he himself didn't partake in any activities that could be injurious to his health. His habits were meticulous. He was the only adult I knew who didn't drink or smoke or chew tobacco, and as a result, his pearly whites had remained untainted, alarming in their brightness. And while he may have been overly controlling with his own dental hygiene, he always kept boiled sweets in his pockets for children. Still, he terrified me.

I once saw him and Begum stood up against the side of their house. Her skirt was bunched up around her hips, and his trousers were down by his knees. He was pressing himself against her in the most hideous way. Begum's blouse was unbuttoned all the way down to her navel, and he had one hand inside her brassiere, and the other, tugging at her hair like a wild animal. It was the look on Begum's face that scared me most – the look he was making her have. It made me understand that no matter how soft Kedar was on Begum, he had a power over her like no other.

Understand: it wasn't the visible act of sex that offended me. As I said earlier, we don't flutter our lashes at that sort of thing in Fountainville. Our houses are nothing more than big barns, offering little privacy, so a child's first experience of sex is often listening to her parents' fumble around in one corner of the room. I was the last of my brood, but my parents still went at it fairly regularly. I knew the sounds of sex well, the surreptitious noises. My mother gasping underneath my father, tugging at him, pushing him off her at the crucial moment – a dubious method of family planning Pastor Joseph suggested to all couples. And I'd also had the pleasure of listening to my six brothers going through varying stages of adolescence in the dark. None of that had anything to do with what I saw Begum and Kedar doing up against the side of their house that summer evening.

Many years later, when I overcame my fear of Kedar, I asked him about his tattoos. 'Well,' he said, 'The serpent is to remind me of desire and temptation, how they always come cloaked in disguises like a trickster, ready to set you on the path to ruination. Which is why I don't whore or drink or smoke or chew tobacco. If a man keeps to his senses, he can't blame nobody but himself for his misfortunes.

'And this one,' he said, stroking the letter B in his skin, 'This one's to remind me that no matter how difficult a place the world is, if you're a lucky son-of-a-bitch, you might find love.'

Kedar had in his employ thirty young thugs who regularly went around bashing in people's heads on his command. They walked around like miniature versions of him – dressed entirely in black, with tattoos on their beefy arms, and silver rings on their fingers. This small army kept control of law and order in Fountainville, leaving Kedar to pursue his philosophical and intellectual ambitions. On the bookshelf at home was a range of texts by stalwart, gloomy-looking, white-bearded men, and whenever there was respite from gangster-work, I'd see Kedar hunched over his desk with a pencil in hand, under-lining passages, which he later transcribed into a notebook he called *The Book of Inspired Ideas*.

Kedar defined himself as a laissez-faire libertarian. He believed that freedom was the only value that was truly human. The principles of free will and free markets, and the freedom to secede from a country that was failing you, were integral to him. He was not a church-going man. He said he liked the stories well enough, but didn't need to sit in a room full of braying idiots every Sunday to figure out what was wrong and what was right. I suppose somewhere in his head he'd reconciled the major contradiction between his actions and his philosophy. When I called him out on that, and pointed out that terror-ising people into a share of every business in town could hardly be classified as laissez-faire behaviour, he said, 'Oh, they're free to go about things another way. It might just be harder is all.'

One thing I'll say in his defence – no matter how

casual and flawed his rationale for living off the proceeds of other people's failings ('No one's forcing them, Luna,' was his standard refrain) – he had his limitations. On the subject of paedophilia, Kedar was militant. For decades there had been a dual racket of heroin and child-trafficking in the triangle towns of Somaville, Murro and Fountainville, of which we were the apex. But Fountainville had been declared a no-go zone as far as children were concerned. Anyone attempting to infiltrate or override Kedar's authority on this matter would find themselves dead in a ditch with their manhood removed. 'Castration alone, is too kind an act,' he said, 'for motherfuckers like them.'

Over the years I came to love Kedar almost as much as I did Begum. I took solace in the shade of their togetherness. Whenever I felt myself moving towards the despair that pulled at me, I felt them pulling from the opposite direction. I knew that the great sadness of their lives had been that they'd had no children of their own. Begum told me the problem lay with Kedar (too much weightlifting, she thought). I also knew that after I came to live with them, their sadness had worn itself down to a tiny nub of nothingness. In this way, we buoyed each other up until we forgot that we were once neighbours, that I once had a family that were now lost to me, that there used to be a baby-shaped hole in their life.

And so when Begum had the idea for the greenhouse, it was a revelation she wanted to share with the both of us. Kedar and I lifted her from the chair and dunked her in a trough of cold water, which seemed to have no effect on her because she kept repeating, 'I saw, I saw.' Finally, Kedar poured a finger of whisky in a glass and said, 'I don't care if you don't want this woman, but you better drink it and tell us what the hell it is you saw.'

What Begum learned from that TV show in Papa Davy's house was a miracle. She said that science and the law had now made it possible to have babies without having sex. That one man's sperm combined with another woman's egg could be implanted in yet another woman's womb without any of them ever having to meet.

A woman in the Mainland – Dr Joy Philipose, had been running a clinic for two years where she out-sourced pregnancies. The TV talk show host, adored and syndicated around the world, called it fertility tourism.

'Isn't that what you're doing?' the talk show host asked, 'Offering wombs for rent?'

Wealthy clients from foreign countries, where the science was in place but not the law, were visiting Dr Philipose's clinic in droves. Dr Philipose had become a millionaire, but she sat there as pious as a nun, looking straight at the camera saying, 'This isn't about making money for me. The greatest joy is to help couples who can't have children of their own; to enable the women of my country, who have so little, to have greater freedom in their lives.'

'Don't you see?' Begum said, 'The clever old cow.'

'But who would want to carry a baby that was not their own?' I asked. 'And why?'

'Who do you think, Luna? Who do you think?'

And that's when Kedar lifted Begum to her feet,

water still dripping from her skirt. He put his arms around her waist and led her through a waltz around the living room – their bodies pressed close together, swaying to a music only the two of them could hear.

VIII

All couples, even those deeply in love like Kedar and Begum, sometimes lose each other. It's impossible to say why they go adrift, but you can see when they're going – in their eyes, their bodies, a slackness in the spine. When Begum got angry she retreated like an animal into a cave, utterly ravaged, but pretending to be calm. All it took was a gesture – an extension of kindness by the guilty party towards her, and she'd emerge, all lightness again. Kedar was more complicated: harder to aggravate, harder to bring back.

Over the years I saw Begum and Kedar extend their arms out to each other many times. I didn't worry much about their skirmishes because when the love is strong there's always a rope by which one lover can bring the other back. But things had changed since Mr Owain had come to Fountainville. Begum – always one to look for portents, remembered how he had walked out of the eye of that great April storm unscathed. We lost half our trees in one night. Even the giant alder protecting the fountain had lost all its leaves and many of its branches. People's houses were destroyed, two young boys died, hundreds of cattle and farm animals killed. Nothing of that scale had ever been recorded in Fountainville. And Begum, being Begum, couldn't help but connect the arrival of Mr Owain with the arrival of great change.

'He's looking to fill my shoes,' Kedar said, from the start. 'If he's not poking around in your business, he's poking around in mine.'

Kedar wasn't normally a jealous man. Among the men of Fountainville he possessed the rare quality of self-awareness. His own personal mission had always been for self-actualisation through body, mind and spirit – quite elevated, all considering. And besides, he was a closet feminist. He adored the women in his life – his mother, three sisters, Begum and me.

A lesser man might have struggled with a famous wife – and Begum's stardom was no ordinary thing. She had put Dr Joy Philipose in the shade within a year of opening our clinic. Not only did Begum revive the myth of the Fountain, she brought prosperity to these Borderlands and forced the government in the Mainland to take up all our long-neglected issues. Besides, she made more money in a month than Kedar did in six, but none of this bothered him. He was proud of her, consistently enamoured. If I didn't live with them, I'd think their love was an invention. But there was something about Mr Owain's involvement with the clinic that threatened Kedar.

'I don't trust him,' he said. 'He doesn't look me in the eye. Always so friendly and flirty with the ladies, but the minute I walk in he shuts up.'

'But he's like a brother,' Begum insisted, 'With nothing incestuous going on!' Why are you over-reacting like this?'

She was pleased of course, for Kedar's surge in jealousy because it indicated he still cared who she gave her time to. But it soon became tedious. 'Isn't it possible he just gets along better with me? Isn't that allowed? That someone might just prefer my company to yours, that not everyone we know has to like us equally?'

'Maybe you scare him?' I offered, when I was still foolish enough to participate in their feuds.

'What do either of you know? Walking around with blinkers on! This man is out for me. I've felt it the minute I clapped eyes on him. He wants something from me, and while he's at it, he's taking you all along for a nice song.'

*

If I had to say when everything changed in our town I'd say it began when Mr Owain asked me his big question. For weeks, things at home had been rough. The fights between Kedar and Begum had escalated. There were rumours about Mr Owain and his activities on the other side of town – horrible stories, which I didn't believe but stuck like fungus to the undersides of my skin. He hardly came to the clinic any more, and when he did, he seemed troubled and distracted.

And then he changed everything by asking me a simple question. Just like that, everything altered. He asked on a Saturday, the busiest day at the clinic, when proxies spend all morning with the team for their weekly progress reports, and Begum and I, between us, oversee that the sheets in the greenhouse are changed, the kitchen stock replenished, the bath house and cow-shed are cleaned out and disinfected.

That particular Saturday I remember having woken early because of a dog fight. Begum and Kedar's pet – a brindled mongrel called Jenga, had been in heat for a week, so all the neighbourhood males were vying for her, scraping through the bamboo fence at all times of day with their howls and long, horny faces. Jenga slept outside my bedroom door, and so the duty usually fell upon me, to chase after her suitors in nightgown and slippers, and stick in hand – an act that cut into my sleep and inevitably put me in a bad mood. That morning though, all I felt was the warmth of the green world at the edge of our house. The dew on the leaves, the prickle of toughened grass underfoot. I stood under the blossom tree beside our house, and felt a wild kind of joy, standing in the sun, being alive. Part of my pleasure, I'll admit, had to do with the fact that Mr Owain had said the evening before, that his feelings towards me were becoming soft and confusing, and he had something to ask me.

I took my usual path to the clinic. Through Main Street, where the farmers' wives were setting out their vegetables, past Lester's butcher shop and Wesley Marx's cycle repair shop, past the property of my would-be ancestors – the Philo General Stores – a thriving business run by three rodent-faced men, the sons of my mother's paramour, Mr Philo.

How many times had I walked down this street, then taken the turn at the Glory Hallelujah Teahouse, into the wooded pathway, past the white houses with blue shutters and tin roofs, the Fountainville School, and the Baptist Church on top of the hill? How many times had I dreamed of escaping it? And today, I thought, finally today, I wouldn't want to be anywhere else in the world but here.

That morning I saw Rafi at the teahouse with his usual entourage of animals jostling around in the gutters for the spot closest to him. I hadn't seen him in a while.

He waved me over. 'How are things going for you, missy?'

Rafi's hair had grown sun-bleached and unruly, and his one cloudy eye looked cloudier, befuddled no doubt, from whisky of the night before.

'Tea?'

I nodded. 'Quick, though. Busy day at work today.'

'How's your lover boy doing?' he asked, as he signalled the waiter for another cup. 'Ah, see! Luna, I didn't even know you could blush. A girl like you? Didn't know you had it in you.'

'He's a nice man.'

'You should tell him to keep his nose out of things that don't concern him. I know a few roughnecks who'd like to say hello to him in a dark alley. Better he stick with those hens of yours in the greenhouse.'

'I thought you of all people didn't pay attention

to rumours,' I said, knocking back my cup of tea determinedly.

'And what does Kedar have to say about him? Is he inviting him over for dinner so you can all get to know each other nicely?'

'He's listening to the same horrible people as you are, I suppose.'

'We care about your safety is all, Luna.'

'Well, thanks for your concern. When you have a moment, come and see Jenga. Those dogs won't leave her alone.'

★

Love is a confusing emotion. It arrives from nowhere and attacks your body like a predator – filling and emptying you – changing your every mood until you're quite unsure of what you were before. Till that exchange with Rafi, I had tricked myself into thinking that I had found in Mr Owain the purest of friendships – something inviolable and true. I was angry at Rafi for not being as wise as I expected him to be, and I was angry at myself for not having defended my friend, my love. All the sweetness of the day disappeared. I was left only with the dissonance of screaming children held captive in school for half-day Saturday, and the dull chop chop chop of the hard-working women of Fountainville collecting firewood along the path up ahead.

Inside the clinic – the usual Saturday scene. Proxies stumbling about in their nightgowns with band aids on their veins; the garden staff clearing away leaves and raking sand; Begum in her office going through the menu of the week with Mitsy, the cook. I had half a mind to turn back, disappear, on the wrong side of town, where no one knew me and no one noticed. In hindsight of course, I'd say it was the body's way of anticipating change, of thinking it could keep the status quo by running away or hiding. But I didn't turn away. Instead, I waited for Mitsy to leave Begum's office.

'I'm bloody sick of Kedar interfering in my life,' I said, marching in. 'It makes me so goddamn angry that you both think I'm incapable of making any decisions for myself. As if I don't have the sense to choose my own friends.'

'Sit, Luna,' Begum said. 'Just sit. Now listen to me: We have to sign Chanu Rose today. We've lost too many weeks already waiting about for his highness. Either Mr Owain decides today, or we assign her to one of our many waiting clients, and ask him to kindly leave us in peace.'

'You believe it too, then?'

'Luna, it isn't about belief or disbelief. Do you think I care what a man does in his free time? I like the man. He's sweet. He flatters me. But he's interfering with my domestic happiness and my business. None of this wellness line boutique stuff he promised has worked out. I've broken rules for him, stretched all kinds of regulations, and I've been very patient. He's a ditherer, Luna. He's lost. He doesn't know what he wants, and maybe you think you can help him but I'm not going to sit back while he destroys our relationship. Come on. Let's talk to him together. Figure out a way to keep everyone happy.'

'Fine,' I said. 'But I'll talk to him first.'

★

I waited till late afternoon. Mr Owain usually came for lunch, but it was only three when he finally showed up. Begum had gone home, and most of the proxies, tired, after their lunch of rice and vegetables, had rolled over to sleep. Only Chanu Rose and I were up, waiting.

Chanu Rose washed her hair every Saturday. It was an arduous task because her hair was so long she needed three buckets of water just to rinse it out. She looked younger than twenty-four. She'd spent most of her life in an orchard picking fruit, but her hands and face carried none of the wreckage of too many hours of sunshine, except for a spray of freckles across her nose. She had small breasts and slim boyish hips, which the other proxies constantly made fun of. 'Where's the room for your package, Chanu?' they'd jibe.

To me, Chanu Rose was the most desirable wo-man in Fountainville: she wore trousers, knew how to change car tyres, and had the blackest, quickest eyes that crinkled up in to two little streaks on her face when she laughed. Most desirable of all though was when she set about washing her hair, which she usually kept restrained in two double braids. Afterwards, she'd sit by the fountain twitching her toes back and forth, humming patiently, waiting for the curtain on her back to dry. And it was at this time – when she was her most perfect and self-contained, that I believe Mr Owain desired her too.

I could see Mr Owain watching her from Begum's porch. Chanu looked like a stick figure in a child's painting. The ring of mountains that surround Fountainville seemed to nestle behind her like a delicate row of capital Ms with the bright gold ball of the sun peeking through between them.

I walked over. 'It's not too late,' I said. 'You can still work with her if you decide today.'

Mr Owain took my hand. 'You know I grew up in a place quite similar to this. In the countryside – with forests and fields and mountains. I liked it well enough as a child, but I can't tell you how quickly I wanted to get out of there as a teenager. And now I live in a dreadful city, filled with the meanest little spirits and scarcely a bird in sight. Everything is about how you present yourself – the clothes you're wearing, and the people you know, and what kind of wine you drink, and where you've been on holiday, and I can't tell you how tired of it all I am. To tell you the truth, I came here because I needed an adventure. I wanted to shake myself out of the life I'd been living. When I talked to Cynon and Cei, and they described the journey here, the challenge, I thought that's what *I* want to do. Set myself up for something difficult.'

'Sounds like a strange kind of adventure to me.'

'My father was a difficult man, Luna. I wasn't the son he'd hoped for, which made him more difficult, but he did manage, in his miserable life, to give me one piece of advice worth keeping. He said if I worked hard I could keep all my sins at bay, which was rich of him to say, of course, because he never worked a day in his life, unless you count riding horses and writing letters to solicitors as some kind of employment. In any case, I coasted through life, scattering what little talent I had away, sacrificing very little and fearing everything, and finally turned into exactly the kind of vacuous bastard I'd been running away from: a version of my father.

'I'm trying to change that now. My father died a year ago, and it's as if his leaving has finally given me the space I needed to become the man I've been trying to be. And that's part of what I'm trying to do here: outwit my DNA if I can.'

'I thought you were trying to propagate your DNA.'

He laughed. 'That too, that too.'

Mr Owain was perfectly still for a few minutes except for clenching his fists, something I knew he did when he was nervous.

'There's no easy way to do this,' he said. 'I've been running around and around for weeks now and it's driven me near damn crazy, so I'm just going to come out and ask: Luna, will you be the mother of my child?'

★

The morning I told Begum and Kedar that I was going to have Owain's child is one of those days that will always stay in my mind as a moment when I could have chosen differently. Everything that followed seems like a dream. But that morning – sitting with Kedar and Begum in the wicker chairs on the veranda with the sun leaking through the roof and Jenga curled up by a pillar – I still felt like my life was my own. Even though it threatened to break away from me like an out-of-control goods train, for that moment, I was still holding on to it with everything I had.

When I announced my news they were both silent for a while. Kedar got up from his chair, walked over to me and knelt. He put his head in my lap as if he were a child, my child. He gripped my knees and looked up, still crouching on the floor.

'I know you've made up your mind,' he said. 'So I won't try to talk you out of it. And I know you're a smart girl, so you know what you're getting yourself in to. I just want to make sure you're covered in every possible way. I'll call a lawyer today – you'll need it, just in case things get tricky.'

I kissed the top of his head. 'You know this means you're going to be a grandfather, right? Because I'm not giving the baby up. That's not part of the plan.'

'Does he have romantic intentions?' Begum asked, quietly from where she was sitting.

Kedar got up and dusted off his pants, moving towards Begum because he could sense, as I did, a growing fury.

'And where will you all live then?'

'I suppose I'll go back with him,' I said. 'But not right away.'

'It'll ruin your life. I'm quite sure of it.'

'Isn't it possible to think about bringing a child into the world in a different way? Not for society or family or loneliness or mortality. Not for money, and certainly not for the mad biological need to replicate yourself. But only because you meet some-one who convinces you otherwise? He's making me reconsider something I've always feared. Doesn't that count for anything? Regardless of whether our relationship remains platonic...'

'Platonic,' Begum interrupted, dumbly. 'Platonic? What sense does that make, Luna?'

'Just because you've never been a mother, and that's been your life's great thwarted ambition, please don't spoil it for me.'

'That's enough,' Kedar said. 'Let's not do this.'

I shouldn't have walked off, but I did. I went straight to the clinic and met Owain there.

'Right,' Dr Willis said. 'All we need are some eggs and some swimmers.' He prepared the first round of drugs for my stimulation and sent Owain off into a darkened room with a cup.

That night Begum came to me the way she used to when I first moved there. I kept my back to her, facing the wall. She said of course she wanted me to have children; that her wish for me was the same as any parent's – for me to marry a man worthy of me, to have a family, be happy.

I should have turned to her and said something reassuring – about how for years I'd seen women come and go from our clinic, swearing I would never do that to my body, not for love or money. And here was this unexpected stranger who had entered my life and changed all my ideas. Wasn't that something? But all I did was say to the cold stone wall: 'It's done.'

IX

Rafi found me at the house the next morning as I was setting off for the clinic. He looked as though he'd had a rougher night than mine — his clothes were shredded, his arms and legs bruised.

'Did you fall in a ditch?' I said. 'What's the point of that walking stick if you don't use it?'

'The news is terrible,' he said, reaching for me with his good arm. 'Oh God, Luna, the news is so very terrible.'

I ran to find Begum but she wasn't in the house. She must have left early. Jenga was jumping with mad delight, grabbing hold of Rafi's leg with her front paws. Normally he would have clubbed her one to the head and she would have settled at his feet in devotion. Not today.

The world is automatically transformed. Isn't it the way? Even the morning call of the birds, which I always interpreted as a song of insistence, of belonging, was now cacophony – the very trees, shrieking in disbelief. The sun was harsh, and all along Main Street, I suddenly felt visible again. I could feel eyes boring into me, although no one could know, not yet. Clothes were drying on washing lines, and roosters were shuffling about making their usual racket. Pastor Joseph, who was buying vegetables with his servant, saw me and raised his hand grandly in a papal-style greeting. I must have had tears in my eyes but could feel nothing except a deadness in my veins, the need to lay myself on the ground, to sleep. To forget. To wake to a different world.

Begum was at the fountain. She was wearing her official robes, the ones she brought out for special functions – a long white dress clinched at the waist with a velvet tasselled belt, emeralds at her throat. When she dressed like that she was her most beautiful self – Goddess-like, overflowing. She was pouring water from the silver cup across the marble slab, washing the surface clean with her fingers. The branches of the alder tree above her were filled with thousands of prayer-flags – so many white-ribboned hopes of mothers-to-be. Watching her, I was for a moment, taken back to childhood. A scene exactly like this one: standing with my mother in the shade, looking at Begum go about her routine. 'Isn't she wonderful, Ma?' I said. And my mother, holding me by the shoulders: 'More wonderful now that she's got those fertility gods to stop being so generous with me.'

Begum looked up and smiled. 'We've neglected the old ways for too long, don't you think? Go change. We should prepare for your first trimester. I'd like to do this properly.'

She knew nothing. How was it possible that she, who was so steeped in signs and portents could know nothing? Shouldn't she have felt a cold shadow pass through her body; the very breath taken from her throat? Isn't that what's supposed to happen when two people are connected in a way they were?

I had to tell her the news myself. Rafi had gone to round up the troops. 'There's going to be a ruckus,' he said. 'Best run to keep your hens safe.'

★

We had a funeral in the rain. Before we took his ravaged body to the cemetery we kept the casket in the house – open, so those devils could see what they'd done. It wasn't as difficult as I thought it would be – seeing him lie in a wooden box against satin cushions with his beloved *Book of Inspired Ideas* tucked in his hands. There was a calmness about him even though his face was unrecognisable. The left side had been beaten so savagely it was nothing but crusted pulp. The only symmetry the undertaker could restore was to part his black hair and lavish talcum over his eyes and cheeks and jaw.

There can be no beauty in death. Only diminishing. I saw that. But there was some pitiable redress in the knowledge that his body had suffered the full extent of its mortal decline. He would not grow old. All the careening and pedalling about we do in life was finally over.

When I lost my family I never saw their bodies because they weren't reclaimed. Their disappearance from my life was a continual haunting – as if they'd been lifted off by aliens, or had decided to emigrate to another country without telling me. There was always the half-fear–half-hope that they might suddenly reappear. With Kedar there were no such doubts. His body was like a Braille that held all the brutal marks of his murder. The knife wounds in his chest, the blows from blunt instruments to his head, the repeated kicks to his stomach and groin and legs. It was Rafi who had found him in the gutter – lifted him, covered him in rags and secreted him away to Xerxes, the bootlegger. He didn't trust Kedar's thugs, even though they were standing grimly like a row of crows, patting down the towns folk who had come to pay their respects. They were expecting what? A suicide-bomber from a rival gang? Knives? Guns?

How quickly the order of things changes.

Everywhere there was a-whispering. Women ululating in full-throated mourning, beating their big chests, coaxing tears from eyes that needed no coaxing. Begum still in her robes, looking as though she might sink into the earth. The proxies around her in a ring of black – bloated and in full view of the townsfolk for the very first time.

And this: I will not forgive or forget. Marina Duke, the seamstress, who had lived two houses down the street from us for more than twenty years, who brought over biscuits and her prized strawberries every Easter – Mrs Duke scuttling over like a giant crab and spitting on the floor at our feet. 'In the end, God punishes those who meddle in His ways,' she said, eyes glinting crazily. 'You!' she said, shoving and poking the proxies. 'May sin come down upon your families. Do they know how you make a living? Whores, all of you. Nothing but whores.'

Begum looked on benignly as though she could not see nor hear while Kedar's thugs made a show of wrestling Mrs Duke out of the house. But it was too late. She had already cast a tarnish over the last sacred thing.

'We have to prepare, Luna,' Rafi said, pulling me to one corner of the room.

'Bring Begum to the fountain as soon as the funeral is over. She must know that this was done by Kedar's men. Play along now, but make no mistake, these men know everything that's going on. If anyone in this town had the power to kill him, it's them.'

When they began to lift the coffin, I went to stand by Begum, who was still looking on, glassy-eyed, transfixed.

'You,' she said, pointing to Owain, who was one of the pall-bearers. 'You will leave this place now.'

'Begum,' I started, but Owain lifted his hand to silence me. Mr Quintus slipped in to take his place.

'I'm so sorry,' Owain said, moving towards Begum. 'So very sorry, you can't know how much I...'

Begum was unleashed, shrieking, down on her knees, beating her fists on the floor, the hem of her beautiful white dress, dirty and torn.

'Luna,' she screamed, 'I won't lose you too.'

I ran to Owain and slid my father's wedding ring into his palm. It was the only thing I had left of my family.

'Take this and hide,' I said. 'There's going to be a war.'

Part Two

I

What am I doing in this country? I no longer remember.

I hear someone speak my name: Owain. Owain. It sounds like a noise from another life. The past is all around me but I cannot speak it. I cannot touch it.

If you ask where I've been, I'll tell you a lie.

It has been a darkness.

If you ask what were the trees like, the weather, did you see snow, or hear birdsong, was the rain warm or cold, did mountains ring close by, or the ocean, I couldn't tell you. Did you lie with woman or man, did you build a house, did you grow fat or thin? I don't know. How can a man lose months of his life you might ask. How can people vanish as if they never existed?

This dream stick produces strange visions. It melts the blood and skin, mixing everything so exquisitely that all you want to do is put your spine to the threadbare mattress and sleep. Sometimes I can feel myself standing outside myself, watching, and it takes hours to get back inside. I must write to Luna, tell her I'm here, to come get me, because I don't know if I have the strength to go to her myself.

If I write, I will not forget. There are only two other people here with me. A sad-faced man who calls himself Earl, and Mala — the wasted beauty, whom we call countess.

If I write, I will not forget.

I remember watching the sun go down like a forest fire in the sky.

I remember a house of twenty-four women.

I remember the fountain.

II

Most nights I am woken by dreams. Running. Screaming. Weapons. Falling down a hillside. Dreams that inevitably have to do with dying. Begum lies next to me on a mattress on the floor, and beside her, Chanu Rose. We sleep together in the drawing room amidst jars and racks of ointments. None of us have been able to return to our beds.

It has been six months since Kedar was murdered, since Owain disappeared. Six months since I started this mad assault on my body, which is changing and growing, just as I feared it would. I feel imprisoned, surrounded by a high stone wall, which is inching closer and closer around me everyday. I have no appetite for food, and am sick all the time. I don't recognise myself. Not my skin, my hair. All of me is different, softer – dare I say it – almost beautiful? Dr Willis says I may have to take to bed for the last month. As if there was anywhere to go!

'Don't look so worried,' he had said. 'You're perfect, you both were. Just one stimulation and plenty of champion swimmers. How could it not be perfect?'

We have abandoned the fountain and the clinic, and moved our equipment into Begum's bedroom for safekeeping. We live among Petri dishes, catheters, ultrasound machines, forceps, scrubs, hairnets, cryoshippers, microscopes, test tubes, suction devices – instruments of torture used to bring life into the world.

I could not do any of it without Begum. I faltered in the beginning, I will not lie. It would not have been hard to kill it. To try and bring us back to where we were before. But Begum wouldn't allow it. She makes potions every day for Chanu and I – mashing forest leaves and honey into all kinds of vile concoctions, which we drink, because they help. She massages our shoulders, reads to us, sings, does everything but talk about what has happened.

I wish she would speak: say, *I told you so, Luna. This would be the ruin of our lives.* But what need is there to speak aloud what everyone already knows?

Fountainville has been under siege. Kedar's thugs installed a rival chief, Marra, who runs the streets with a cruelty I never knew existed. Most of Marra's men were recruited as children during the last War of Secession – abducted, brainwashed, orphaned. Boys. They're just boys who've been wielding machetes and rifles since they were fourteen; forced to kill neighbours and friends to prove their manhood; smear the blood of the dead on their palms. For breakfast they're fed cocaine, which they take through the day so they can remain high-strung and ruthless.

We are in a state of permanent curfew because of these men who have no family, no country, no understanding of remorse. Women who don't stay indoors are carried off and locked in sheds where they are raped, shot, discarded. Children no longer play in the streets because they'd be picked off too – as easily as the panther steals dogs at night. Main Street is a ghost street – only roosters and pigs poke around in the empty gutters, and soon, they too will disappear. At night we sleep in the brief silences between gun shots, and during the day, those who still hope, congregate in the church to cower before their Lord. And this is the world I will bring my child into.

'People of Fountainville,' Marra said, the morning after Kedar's funeral, smiling in that oily, unconvincing way only the most brutal dictators have. 'We are here to help you. This is a new age for your town. My men are here at your disposal to make the transition. Any problem, you ask them. We mean you no harm. We must only make a negotiation with your Lady. If she agrees, you will continue your lives as they were before. If not... if not, we must see. Those who cooperate will be rewarded. Those who resist will experience the full wrath of Marra's Army of Liberation.'

We sent our proxies home immediately, all except for Chanu Rose, who is as far along as I am. She said we might as well put a hatchet in her head if that's what we wanted because if she went home in this state she would soon be dead. Begum and I contacted all the prospective parents to inform them of our altered circumstances. We would do our best, we told them, but could no longer guarantee safe delivery and handover. Litigation was inevitable. We paid the proxies double what they were owed and urged them to find refuge where they could. Rafi helped with their passage through the forests.

We managed to secure the fountain and the clinic for a few days with the help of Rafi and a group of townsfolk. But what could they really do? They were only shepherds and farmers after all. And even if Rafi alone could withstand the attacks of ten men bare-armed, his body wasn't impervious to bullets. The awful truth is that all of it seems inevitable now. Kedar was killed because of the mother lode of Begum's clinic. They had been waiting for him to soften, to turn his attention away, and I had helped them do it. Fools! What do they know about Assisted Reproductive Technology? What do they know about fertility and fountains for that matter?

And there has been nothing in the news. For all

our world-famousness, we are back in the red zone without any sign that the Mainland is aware of what's going on. If they knew, I don't believe they'd send troops to rescue us. They'd shift their gaze elsewhere – look above into the higher mountains or at those valley people suffering in the plains. There is always some place else that can make a greater claim on suffering.

Marra came to our house dressed in a suit. He handed Begum a card before sitting down.

'So,' Begum said, 'these days even terrorists have business cards.'

'It's very simple,' he said, 'you keep a fourth of everything you were making and continue to run the place exactly as it was before, with full protection offered by us. My men will step back. We have other wars to fight in the Borderlands. Your streets will go back to normal. All will be as it used to be.'

Marra was a slight man with a scar for every battle he'd fought etched into his face like the twigs and string that line a bird's nest. He had long, musical fingers, which he cracked earnestly as he spoke, and when he listened, he leaned in towards you, as if to better receive your words.

'Take it all,' Begum said. 'I have no interest in running my clinic for other people. And you haven't the first clue how to do it yourself.'

'You are not irreplaceable,' Marra smiled. 'I'm only offering it to you as a courtesy. I know that the people of this town pay attention to customs and old stories. I'd like them to continue to have their stories. Stories are good, aren't they? Otherwise what will people know about themselves? How will they understand their lives? You do an important job, Madam. But not as important as mine. You have my card, and a week to make up your mind.'

'You killed my husband. What about that story? Want me to forget about that?'

'Your husband was killed by his own men because he no longer served them as a leader. You understand well, I think, the laws of survival. Do not make me teach them to you. Good day.'

Rafi thinks if we can smuggle Begum across to the Mainland she could get in touch with news channels about what is happening. He says the centre will be forced to take action because Begum is a public figure.

'I was a public figure as long as Kedar was lining the pockets of the Minster of Health and Family Welfare. Now I'm just another woman from the Borderlands with a sad story to tell.'

'But what else will we do,' I say, 'If we can't defend the fountain, we've lost everything.'

'Haven't we already lost, Luna?'

III

Luna. You want to know about the place I am now? I tell you it is rife with sadness.

The widowed countess, Mala, runs it. She fills our pipes and sweeps the floors, and smiles as though she invented the world but I know she has her own history with sadness. I heard she lost her husband terribly. After he died she could not find her way back.

Do you know about a woman's honour Mala asks. They would have me burn, jump into his dying flames to prove my worth. I am done with asking the earth to swallow me. Look – she lifts up the hem of her skirt, displaying a silver anklet on the delicate stem of each leg. Once I had rooms full of treasures. Now I have only this. A woman is nothing without a man to protect her.

The days pass like this – in chatter and smoke.

The Earl of Sadness has his woes too. He's telling us about his two sons who went hunting in the forest and were captured by a bandit and his gang. Did they ask for a ransom? No – that would be easily done? Did they want his Earldom? He would gladly give it. What they wanted was the Earl's fair daughter. He has only one. Those rascal bandits wanted to barter, to parley. We'll give you your sons for your daughter. What a dilemma the Earl has! What's a man without his sons? What's a father without a daughter?

Do you have children, Knight? The countess interrupts. If you don't, you can't possibly understand any of it. You're a childless charlatan. What do you know what it means to lose? I had a child but he was born wrong. I had a husband but he was killed. Who do you have to live for but yourself?

Hush, The Earl says, Do you want to hear the rest of it? The question is hypothetical of course – it doesn't matter if you don't have sons or daughters. The point is would you offer one in exchange for the other? Think about it. I've thought and thought, and I have to say I'd have to let my line end with me but I won't give up my girl.

The countess seems happy with his reply – she'd purring like a cat, blowing smoke out of her nostrils.

You two should get together, I say. A man of means, and a woman without protection. Together you could breed kingdoms of sadness.

Shut it, Knight. Get out of the way.

No, wait. Sorry. I want to help. Please don't misunderstand. It's just, I'm sad too. But I want to help. Let me go to the borders of the world, to the desolate mountains – to find those bandits who hold the Earl's sons. Let me save them. I'm not a man who shies away from a challenge.

But first, Countess, fill up my pipe and let me lie down one last time. And you have maidens – twenty-four of them, you say? Let them attend to me with meat and drink and fire and a bath, and if they could saddle up my horse, I would be ever-grateful. When I wake I will be whole again, my flesh bright as what is brightest.

IV

I have been waiting for a sign from him, something to say he's safe, that he thinks of us. And as if to answer me, last night the heavens opened up with a thunderstorm of such magnitude and fury, it almost rivalled the April storm that first ushered him into our lives.

Imagine – three women sitting on a stone floor, swaddled in blankets, looking through the window grilles at the sky, which has turned into a sheet of steel, and the rain coming down in sharp slices of hail like millions of tiny daggers falling to the earth. Begum, in the aftermath of her grief, is thinner, her hair overrun with grey. On either side of her Chanu Rose and I, who could be her daughters; one with her beauty, the other with her determination. We sit for hours, crouched in this way – Chanu and I with our big bellies and skinny legs propped over pillows, Begum between us.

It's impossible to know whether to keep our eyes to the sky or the veranda outside, where hundreds of animals and birds have gathered to take shelter. There are the usual – cows and goats, rabbits and pigs, but there are also birds as I've never seen, huddled together in a flock – jungle-fowl, lapwings, egrets, kestrels, flycatchers, hoopoes, cormorants and Pariah Kites – each contributing its own startled cry to the collective.

They're waiting for Rafi, who will not come. He sleeps outside most nights, keeping watch, but yesterday he went back to the forest. 'I get my strength from the trees,' he said. 'I'm no good to you without my strength.'

At four in the morning there's a sudden lull in the storm, a softening. Lightning no longer cracks open the sky, and the wind and rain has subsided from a mad howling to a whisper.

'Come,' Begum says, 'Let's go to the fountain.'

We ready ourselves in the dark, fending off the cold with layers of scarves and water-proof sheeting. I fetch Kedar's pistol from the safe and slip it into the pocket of Begum's skirt. Jenga whimpers in disapproval.

'You don't have to come if you don't want to,' Begum says, stroking Jenga's furrowed head.

'Torches?'

Chanu hands them out, one for each of us.

'Okay, now keep close.'

Begum steps out, and immediately, there is a terrific screeching. Every bird on the veranda takes to the sky like a magic carpet of squawking feathers. It's a wonder there aren't any collisions.

We stifle giggles. 'Heavens,' Begum says.

We flatten ourselves against the wall. Ridiculous – a trio of gargantuan mummies.

Silence again.

'Follow me.'

Outside our world lies in broken splendour. It's as if giants had come out to play during the storm. Blocks of concrete and granite flung about like matchsticks. Hundred-year-old trees uprooted as though they were turnips. Main Street looks like a long, splintered backbone in the dark. Everywhere the smell of wet. Shuttered shops gleam like painted toenails, and all along the street there are clusters of tin roofs and thatch, leaves and branches. We move through the debris in single file. Jenga following at our heels, close as a ghost.

The greenhouse looks so ordinary and small in its abandoned state. Something about all this dereliction warms me, fills me with hope.

The Mainlanders believe that only from great destruction can things begin anew. In this, they understand something we can't. Their gods are different from ours; they sanction a wilful subjugation to fate, to the idea of cycles, which necessitates that darkness and light are interchangeable. They are better equipped to deal with disasters because of their philosophy, and by that same measure, when others are suffering, it's easier for them to look away.

It's their fate, they say, *so they must withstand it.*

Funny, Begum, who was always such a big believer in destiny has stopped talking about it. But I suppose when we imagine our lives in the future, it's natural not to think of the ways it can unravel, to focus instead on all the luminosities we feel we are deserving of.

Chanu and I hold hands, our boots crunching across the gravel. We have no more need for torches as our eyes have grown accustomed to the lack of light. Everything comes alive in the shadows. The alder tree has lost every one of its leaves. It stands bare and proud, like an enormous inky thumbprint against the dawn. Begum is clearing the mess away from the marble slab, her body stooped over from the waist, sweeping. She picks up the silver cup and pours water over the slab, wiping the dirt away with her hands. All around her, a soggy rug of leaves and twigs.

'Come,' she says, gesturing with one hand, 'Drink.'

Chanu and I kneel gently in the mud with our hands cupped, letting the cool water stay enclosed in our palms for a few seconds before bending our necks backwards like swans to drink. We drink and we drink the sweetest water we've drunk in weeks.

'I've decided to make a deal with Marra,' Begum says. 'It kills me to do it, but you're right, Luna. If we want to save the fountain, I can't see any other way.'

Chanu nods slowly.

'Kedar would have wanted it,' I say.

'Perhaps. I don't know if I can think about that anymore. Some days I just want to be done with it all. But I have you two to think about, and the two you'll bring into the world, and all the women and men of Fountainville who have come to me and told me their dark fears, begging me to bargain with this terror of a man, so they can pick up their lives and go about their days as they used to.'

★

We make our way back at daybreak. Nothing stirs. Not Marra's men, nor the townsfolk. Where is everyone hiding? In the far fields that lie outside Fountainville, there are farmers out with their ploughs thanking God that they are poor and unworthy of Marra's attentions. They have nothing to give, and so they have been allowed to carry on toiling through their difficult lives. Now, with the sun rising over the eastern ridge, the wreckage of Main Street is more visible. The sign for the Ambition Computer Centre lies in a heap outside the building, the windows are smashed and most of the roof has caved in. The Glory Hallelujah is a ruin of blue shutters and wooden tables. The entire street, from where we stand, looks broken, like a scene from one of those war-ravaged cities we will never visit, but know intimately because of its degradations.

As we labour our way up the hill, Jenga suddenly sprints forwards with renewed energy. Rafi is back. He's standing on the veranda with his usual menagerie.

On the stoop, there is a stranger. He's smoking with his legs stretched out in front of him. I can tell it's not him, even from this distance. Even if there's something familiar about the way he locks his legs, there is nothing of Owain in this man. No matter how badly my heart needs this hope, my eyes will not give it.

This man is stocky and dishevelled. I walk faster, striding past Begum and Chanu Rose, so I can see better. He has long blond hair tied low in a ponytail, and a beard of many days. Who is this lump of a man wearing a ridiculous camouflage outfit? I quicken my pace, panting. Now I am within direct sight of him, I see he is beautiful. Shockingly so, with deep green eyes and golden skin.

'There you are,' Rafi says, casting his one good eye over our mud-spattered clothes. 'You won't believe who I have here. Come from the Mainland, if you please, with a driver and an SUV, asking for the world-famous Fountainville Clinic. They were lost in the forest. Would've been dead by now, if I hadn't saved him. Damn nearly stepped on a monocled cobra! Although, that might have been preferable to one of Marra's men.

'Go on,' Rafi says, prodding the stranger's back with his walking stick. 'You better tell them.'

'I'm Leo,' the stranger says gruffly, standing up,

extending his hand.

When he stands he's transformed – not the crouching figure he was a moment ago, but broad-shouldered, powerful, almost menacing.

'This ugly giant tells me you were the last ones to see my boyfriend.'

V

She comes everyday and I can do nothing to make her go away. What is her name? I knew it once. She comes wearing a dress of yellow brocaded silk, riding a bay horse with a mane that touches the ground, and a saddle of gold. She asks what kind of man I am. I try to speak, tell her the journey I've been on, but she silences me.

Shame, she shouts. Shame, shame for deceiving us. Give me back my ring, traitor!

I tell her it's the only thing I have left in the world.

You don't deserve it, she says, turning away on her horse. You don't deserve a good thing for all you have deceived us.

I try to get my friends to speak up for me. We are friends now — the Earl of Sadness and the Widowed Countess.

Why don't you tell her what kind of man you really are?

What should I say? That I'm the worst kind – arrogant, afraid, always seeking someone who might get the better of me, or I the better of him. The kind of man who proves himself in showdowns and useless acts of prowess.

The weaker we are the more we must do it. Can't you understand? I was doomed from the start because of my father, and his father before. But one day I arrived in a strange land, on the day after a miraculous storm. And a man, who was no smaller than two men of this world with one good foot and the other lame, one good eye and the other blind, led me to the fountain. Near the fountain was a house of twenty-four maidens who were lovely, and who laughed at everything I said. And when I saw them, I coveted all that was not mine, and could never be mine. I wanted the impossible. I thought I would die from the wanting.

It was only when she came and rescued me, whispered in my ear, There's a way, there's always a way. She saw every good thing in me and magnified it a thousand times. When I was with her I wasn't myself. Or rather, I was the best version of myself. She led me to the fountain to drink, and the fountain changed me.

VI

'You can't be serious.'

This is what Leo repeats again and again.

'Nothing about me? He didn't mention me once? And yet I know everything about you.'

He looks pityingly at me and Chanu Rose, at our swollen stomachs.

'Tell me what did he say? That his dad was a horrible man? That he needed to change his life? That he got tired of waiting for the right person? It's all bloody Cei and Cynon's fault, parading Neneh around like the latest accessory. First it was marriage vows, now it's family and children. It's all going terribly wrong for us.'

We are in Begum's drawing room drinking tea. This is not the man I had imagined for Owain.

When he revealed his secret to me – months ago, during one of those rambling teatime rituals – he'd stumbled through the story of his confused sexuality, from boys to girls to boys again, blushing and blustering. I had placated him, told him I'd always known, that it changed nothing. But I had expected a different kind of lover, someone intelligent, urbane, soft. Not this opinionated ruffian.

'We broke up because I didn't want to have children. Sorry, but two men cocktailing their sperm and getting some unfortunate woman to bake it in her oven, I don't understand. What's the point? When we first met he wasn't like that at all. He just wanted to travel, to live. I don't know what happened. Societal bloody conformism, is what. All of a sudden it was let's cut out dairy products and hire a life coach and invest in third world micro-credit basket-weaving. Really! His problem was the desire to be nobler than he actually was. I was the only one who saw him for what he was, and I said it straight. But he had grander ideas for himself, stupid bugger.'

I know what Begum is thinking. So, it's true. It's all

true. The rumours of Owain going off with young men in town, the experiments with opium. The reason why he disappeared for days at a time without offering any explanations. And if that was true, then what else was?

'Mr Owain left Fountainville after my husband was murdered. His involvement in the murder was initially suspected by some, but now the general consensus is that he was a coward who ran away when things got tough.'

I interjected. 'He left because you demanded it.'

'I think, given my state at the time, and the evidence, I can be excused for wanting him out of my sight. But to disappear for so long? When you're in this condition? What kind of a man does that?'

'I thought he'd have gone home. We haven't heard a thing from him since he left. I thought he would have sent word, something.'

'Well I haven't heard either,' says Leo. 'I was trying to play it cool, keep my distance. But it's been six months and no missives of misery-me confusion, so I thought I'd better take a few weeks off and come see what's going on.'

Rafi, who has been pacing up and down the veranda with his walking stick, enters now, struggling to fit through the frame of the door.

'He hasn't gone very far. If my spies serve me well, he's nearer than we think. Mr Leonard, you may have noticed we are going through difficult times. There's a lot of work to do, so I'll be asking if you could set aside the issue of your vulnerable heart, and Luna, this goes for you too.'

'Yes, well, it's all been a bit rock and roll for me as you can imagine. I need half an hour to sort things out at work. I've sort of abandoned them in the middle of an important case.'

'What is it that you do?' asks Begum.

'Oh, this and that. Mostly I'm a barrister for human rights and war crimes. If I didn't have to support that tosser, I'd like to give it all up and do fashion photography.'

★

I am given the task of holding the video camera and training it on Leo while he puts on what he calls his posh voice and speaks about the fate of Fountainville and the neighbouring border towns. Before we begin, he unties his ponytail and releases a mane of raggedy blond hair, gives it a swift brush with his fingertips and scrunches it up and out of sight again. He catches me staring and grins.

I sweep the camera across the house capturing Begum and Chanu in the corner with a few other townswomen looking frightened, the Ridge in the distance, then moving to the courtyard where Leo is hunched, as if awaiting a missile, still wearing his ridiculous camouflages.

I'm here in the midst of a dramatic unfolding.... His words blur as he speaks.

The town of Fountainville in the far northeast, struggling for its autonomy since 1947, making it the longest running insurgency in the country.... The remarkable story of Begum Azad, whose husband, Kedar Azad, was overthrown in a bloody coup seven months ago... once flourishing economy, a multi-million industry of outsourcing pregnancies lies in tatters... the town is in control of rebel forces... Marra's Army of Liberation... people barricaded in their houses... the fountain, key to the town's welfare, is under their control... impasse for these people who have too long been forgotten by their own government and the world... this is a plea to the international community... they need your help...

Listening to him this way, through a magic lens, which distorts people into different beings, I begin to see how it must have been for Owain to love this man. There is no space for doubt in Leo's body. At every joint and sinew he is compressed, tightened, ready to jump and roar in defence. He is not someone who oscillates between desires. One of those strange beings of the world who seem to have entered it complete, with opinions and ideals in place. When he speaks, it is without the slightest trace of humility, no fear of ridicule, no faltering. How hard to be noble compared to that.

'All right, Luna?' Leo asks, stepping over to take the camera from me and replay what I've just shot.

'Not bad. This should do it. You've got a steady hand.'

Leo's duffle bag is bursting with technological toys, each one of them tiny, precise, and capable of things I never thought possible. A satellite router, pen camera and handheld GPS system.

'Pretty amazing, huh? Proper secret agent material. Never leave home without it.'

Within a few hours it is all ready to be dispatched: press releases, videos, photographic evidence, testimonials. All of it sent across cyberspace. Click click click. Gone. Our news in their inboxes.

We have an hour before darkness sweeps in.

'Can't you stay, Luna?' asks Chanu. A rare request. 'Let them go. It isn't safe.'

It's only a half-hearted plea. She knows me too well. Rafi will lead Leo and I past the Northern Forest Ridge, in the direction of Somaville, where he believes Owain is being sheltered. We don't know what to expect. The worst, obviously. Amnesia, madness, near-death.

Begum packs a selection of ointments for me. 'You'll know what to give him when you see him.'

★

We walk for two hours using the inner routes, away from the river and road checkposts. I lift my legs up and down like a wind-up toy, propelled forward by the thud thud sound of Rafi's boots ahead of me, and Leo behind. We are like three bats in the forest. All around the dark night: ravines on either side, trees that arch up like demons and fill the sky.

The forest at night is a place of nightmare or dream. Spirits, if they roamed, would march about in a place like this. Without Rafi, I wouldn't have dared it.

On and on. The trees are like pencils, long and thin, black and sharp. Coming at me. Coming at me. I'm tired. There's no use denying it. I want to sit down here and be done with it all. How long to keep going when the earth is calling, saying, rest your feet, come back to me?

'Here,' I say, stopping, leaning against Leo. 'Let's stop here for the night. I can't go further.'

Water-legs. Darkness.

They tell me later I was burning up with fever. Delirious. Talking about the end of the world, and being imprisoned in a wall of stone. Where is he? I kept asking. Tell him I can't breathe. These stones are killing me. And the fire. If he doesn't come, they'll burn me. Already they're stacking up the logs. In another time, they would have called me witch. Now it's harlot. Shall I just offer my neck?

It used to be that a human head brought good fortune to the village.

Take my tendons please, and end it. Let me close my eyes and fall. Just fall.

VII

Is this death then? Nothing like I expected it to be. No bright lights or running sepia footage, vignettes of my brief tumultuous life. No crushing against my lungs, no music. Nothing except this wide-open field with indigo birches studding the periphery like a row of soldiers.

In the middle of the field there is a dog gnawing on a bone. Milly, is that you? Can it be? Milly, my greyhound, dead, fifteen years or more, chewing on a meaty bone.

Is this childhood then? Am I returned to that difficult place after all this? I would rather be dying than falling backwards in time.

Hello there, Earl? Are you still here? Are we still in the place we were yesterday?

Everything is amiss. Countess, you have abandoned me, I'm sure.

Earl — I hear loud shrieks in the forests of my dreams. I cannot say if I'm awake or asleep but I'm moving across the sky on a winged horse looking down over the most desolate place you ever saw.

In one corner is childhood — Milly, Mama, Father. All chewing on bones. But I cannot stay with them. I'm traversing mountains, still on my winged horse, being separated from every familiar thing I know.

Ahead of me is the most enormous cliff. In the middle of the cliff is a grey rock, and in that rock is a snake.

Earl — it is a terrible snake, smooth-scaled and brown with ragged yellow bands along its body. It sleeps in fields and termite mounds, in rodent burrows and rice fields, amongst piles of brick and rubble. It moves through the world like a long pale-throated worm. But here it is terrifying — angry, provoked — raising its body, hissing, striking, opening its hood.

A hood, Earl! A snake with an eye in its hood. And with this one eye, it watches the world.

And who does this snake hold captive? A white lion. Purest of pure. Trapped between the snake and the long fall down the cliff. Every time the lion tries to move, the snake raises its body, spreads its hood, opens its eye, and hisses.

If I could just kill the snake, cut its body in two, and free the lion — my life would be mine again. But I know no way of doing it. Can you lend me your sword, Earl? Can you help me? I cannot find my way out of these woods.

There's more, Earl. There's a woman who's going to be burned. A woman trapped in stone. She says she loves me, and I believe her. They'll burn her alive if I don't save her. They're preparing a pyre in the forest, stacking logs of wood one on top of the other, fetching the fuel, the match. Every time I get close to her, she disappears. I cannot see her face. Only smoke. And the pipe is empty.

Someone is walking home. I must follow.

VIII

When I come to, I see a high ceiling above. Around me, peeling walls with animal heads hung crookedly along them. I can feel the hard cold floor pushing through the thin mattress, pressing into the flesh of my back. Somewhere to the left, there's a room where someone is making a droning noise along with a relentless knock knocking against a wooden door.

It is a chieftain's house. I can tell, because of the ceremonial altar at the entrance, and the wooden effigies that line the balustrade, which rings down grandly on the far side of the room. Not so long ago, human heads would have been strung like lanterns outside this house. Our people used to believe that a man's soul resides in his head, that when you cut off a head, you receive the potency of its soul. But then the Baptists came and told us that man's soul is ever-lasting. And no amount of head-chopping will bring you luck or rain or keep diseases away.

Before a warrior could decapitate a victim, he had to ask their name.

How civil.

Luna. My name is Luna Anto.

Take it then, and string it to your name. Borrow my spirit for your own. Kill my strength and become stronger.

A man stands over me with milky eyes. His face is full of tattoos. He is old and bent and bare-chested. All over his arms, shoulders, face and ribs, there are tattoos of tigers and dragons. Around his neck, a single chain threaded with a line of brass heads.

'Hello,' he says. 'I'm Sabina's father.'

'Sabina?'

'She came to make a baby in your clinic. Do you remember? My daughter. She's the saviour of the house.'

'Sabina, the proxy? What's she to do with anything?'

'She knows where he is,' he says, pointing to my stomach. 'Your baby's father. It's a terrible place. They've gone there now. I have a daughter there. Mala. She went crazy after her husband died. Sabina tried to bring her back, but Mala didn't want to be saved.'

I try to raise myself up on my elbows. Blood-rush. Gold flecks stinging the backs of my eyes. I remember now, months ago, a wasted woman appearing at the gates of the clinic. Sabina's sister. The two of them on the bench exchanging whispers and money. And Owain, afterwards, asking to see those places.

'Stay,' the old chief says. 'You stay here.'

His voice is a low rustle. The sound of leaves scratching. Dead grass. I think of my father. His patience. 'Please,' I say, 'Don't leave me.'

'Don't worry. They'll bring him back. They'll beat him in the head if they need to, but they'll bring him back.'

'But where's he been for six months? What kind

of state is he in?'

'You are the Lady's daughter, isn't that right? The Lady of the Fountain? If you have her magic, you'll be able to heal them. It's the only chance they have.'

I stare into his weathered face. How much the world has changed for him. I cannot imagine the countless things he has witnessed, endured.

'How do you know these things?'

The old chief cracks a toothless smile. Years of tobacco-chewing have made his mouth an estuary of red rot.

'I know, I know,' he giggles. 'I know too many things. Sabina, my daughter, she spies. She tells me everything. She loves Rafi. Rafi loves her.'

★

They enter like beggars − clothes ripped, hair matted, eyes running, smelling of something animal, something broken. Three of them. Owain, Mala, and a dark crippled reed of a man they call the Earl of Sadness, from whom they will not be separated.

They don't know us, barely register their new surroundings.

'Countess,' Owain keeps saying to Mala, 'another pipe.'

He is wearing my father's ring. I can see it from where I lie.

Pain in my back. Ankles swollen. I feel useless. 'Owain,' I say, 'Owain, come here.' But he doesn't know who he is or where he is.

'Please,' he says, looking straight at me, recognising nothing. 'Don't ask me anything. I can't betray her.'

The knocking sound from the child's room is overpowered by new commotion. Sabina is all efficiency, dragging in wood for the stove. Barely a word to me except for, *Luna, stay, rest.* Impossible to tell she's had a baby two months ago, but for the puckered ring of fat around her middle.

'Did it go okay?' I ask, 'the handover?'

She grimaces. 'Baby Hank is thriving. I have pictures from Mr and Mrs Mullins. I'll show them to you later perhaps.'

Rafi is out by the well hoisting water. I want to

interrogate him about his love affair, the sly devil. But he knows I know, and he is heaving, bucket after bucket of water.

There's a symmetry to their industry. Three on three. Leo – in and out of the house with buckets. Sabina by the wood fire, heating cauldrons. Mala, Owain and the Earl, whispering on the floor.

The old chief sits on a tree stump in the courtyard watching the proceedings like an eagle. Curled in his lap, a black cat, whose fur he tugs this way and that.

'Papa,' Sabina barks, 'Rest-time now.'

He pretends not to have heard, breaks a lump of tobacco in his palm, pops the ball into the back of his rotten mouth, and waits, defiantly.

'Put on a shirt and go to sleep,' she yells again, 'and shut that child up. As if there wasn't enough to do.' The old chief throws the cat off his lap and shoots a stream of red through his gums, making a pool of betel juice on the courtyard floor.

'You shut up,' he mutters, hitching up his shabby trousers and limping off in the direction of the child's knocking.

'It's not the child's fault,' he says, as he passes me. 'His mother was given the wrong medicines when he was inside her. It's not his fault he's wrong in the head.'

'Okay, okay, just go,' Sabina says.

'Now,' she says, steering Leo towards Owain. 'Pick him up. Let's start with the easy one.'

'O,' Leo says, stroking his shoulder. 'O, it's me!'

Nothing.

'Hey love, it's me!'

They look beautiful together. One blond the other dark. One expansive, the other, tender, contained.

Rafi pats Leo on the back softly. 'He doesn't know you.'

He hauls Owain up from under his arms and makes him stand.

'Take off his clothes,' Rafi tells Leo.

I looked for it, of course I did. How could I not? Some glimmer of recognition between them.

Surely the body remembers its old loves? And if one should press close against you, removing the very clothes from your skin, wouldn't he carry his own special smell?

Isn't memory connected to those scents we hold within our bodies like pathways, tracts of land, territory. When I think of Owain, I think of rain, smashed flowers and leaves, damp rising from the mud, woodsmoke. Every time he held my hand, it was this. And when we lay together, holding each other on the sterile clinic beds the night Dr Willis set all this in motion, I curled into the bark of his body, and it was inside him. That smell – after the storm.

And with Leo, were there different memories, different smells? Are some stronger than others? I watched them, telling myself if there was even the slightest spark of remembrance, if Owain looked at him a certain way, I'd.... what? Give them my baby? Allow them their happily ever after? I couldn't do it. It went against any kind of sense. All those proxies I'd known, who had subjected their bodies to the prison of pregnancy, given up their babies without ever touching or seeing them. How did they tolerate it? It was as if all they'd been were temporary shelters. As if those nine months of pre-birth were nothing. How must it be to know that a child born from you is walking the world but doesn't know you?

I couldn't give my baby up even if I didn't love it yet. Even though I'd been prepared to drag it out of me.

In any case, there was no need for grand gestures just yet.

Owain doesn't know Leo. He doesn't know anyone. All he wants is a pipe.

'Give me a pipe,' he says. 'Countess, please.'

'Yes, yes,' coos Sabina. 'We'll give you one in a little while. Come with me first. Let me sit you down and wash you.'

★

When they have been bathed and groomed and made to look something human, we lay them down on mattresses at the back of the house and give them cups of milk laced with laudanum to still them a bit. They fall back on pillows, resolute in their togetherness.

News is trickling in. It hasn't been long, but the

world already knows. In certain corners people are taking to the streets with placards and kitchen knives. Leo tells us that our video has gone viral. Half a million hits in less than twenty-four hours. The government has declared an emergency and a curfew has been imposed on the Borderlands. The army has taken over the checkposts and Marra has gone missing.

I unpack Begum's ointments. Heavy glass jars of buttery panaceas.

A boy in a too-small checked shirt and torn shorts comes out to watch. He is eight or nine, barefoot, pale. He must be Mala's boy, Mingus. He stands beside me, swaying frontwards and backwards on his splayed feet. There's a wooden spoon in his hand that he waves as if it were a magic wand.

'Is that for me?' I ask.

'No,' he says, 'It's mine. My friend.'

It must be what he uses to knock against the bedroom door. That constant knock knocking – a secret language only he can understand.

'You can watch, if you want,' I say.

I have different kinds of ointments, one for each of them. I begin with Owain, pick up his heels, cracked and dry. I move up his shins, so thin and bird-like. To the knobbly parts of his knees. Groin, navel, belly, nipples, throat, arms, eyelids, nostrils, ear lobes, lips, forehead. I turn him around and begin at his feet again. Sweeping and kneading upwards, to the wide desert of his back, his hair, the tender part of his neck, every inch of skin anointed.

Mingus parks himself on the floor a little away from me, looking over every once in a while to see what I'm doing. I want to put socks on his feet, give him a proper shirt and trousers. He has beautiful fingers, solid and shiny as piano keys. He holds the kitchen spoon in those fingers tapping it this way and that, in a world of his own.

'Mingus,' I call out. 'You want to help me?'

He doesn't hear. Or if he does, pretends to ignore me. Tip tap, tip tap.

I wonder what it must be to have a child like this. I used to think that only the most optimistic people had children, or the most short-sighted. Anyone who actually thought it through logically would see it for what it was: a dissolution of individual spirit. You see the failings of the world around you and still you think, I will bring another soul into it, and it will be all right, they will thrive and blossom and make something of life.

And then there's love. Love changes your mind too.

If I hadn't met Owain I wouldn't be here, in this condition. Love suspends disbelief. Love is what a child like Mingus could bring, although I don't think Mala sees it that way, or Sabina. Only the old chief is mad about the boy.

After his nap the chief emerges with a mug of sweet black tea for me and a banana for the boy.

'You have to peel it, and break it into two halves,' he says. 'And no part of it can be brown. He's very particular.'

Mingus's face creases into delight. He takes the peeled banana from his grandfather and jumps up, running towards his room in a strange giraffe-like gallop.

'Have you thought about what you're going to name your son?' the chief asks. 'You know you're going to have a boy?'

★

I don't know how many days I spent in the old chief's house. A week? Two? You lose track of time. I remember my body growing further and further away from me, the continuous swell and press, having to lie down and rest between sessions with Mala, Earl and Owain.

I remember sunny days in the courtyard and the contented hum of an overfull house. Our duties were divided according to our capabilities. Rafi brought in the wood and water. Sabina cooked. Leo washed the dishes and monitored the various twitches and chirrups of his gadgets, informing us of the latest developments. The old chief entertained us with his banjo. Despite having few teeth left, he still knew how to turn a song.

Day by day Mingus shed some of his shyness. He

was a funny boy. Sometimes his eyes would fill up with tears for no reason that I could understand. Other times he would chortle to himself as though an invisible pair of arms were tickling him. Often, while I was administering ointments, he'd come over with his wooden spoon, pretending to be a doctor and tap the patients on their knees. Boink, boink, boink, waiting for a reaction.

Sometimes the world returns to us so imperceptibly, it's difficult to locate the seams, the exact junctures where things begin to change.

I can't tell you when the ointments started to work their magic. I only know it began, not in the knees, but in the eyes. Owain would say later, that it was like a curtain slowly being drawn. An uncovering, a resuscitation.

It took a while before he could say my name. The recognition fluttering, hiding, reappearing.

One day he slid my father's ring off his finger and pressed it in my palm. 'You really should take this back. Thank you for letting me have it.'

If I could have managed it, I would have got down

on my knees to give praise to every God and spirit I knew. But I was well past the stage of such acrobatics, I just bellowed across the courtyard, 'Rafi, it's time.'

★

Throughout my childhood what I wanted most of all was to escape Fountainville and never return. Every fear I know began when I was a child, and it has taken years for me to confront and vanquish them. Begum tells a story of when I first came to live with her and Kedar, when to add to my staple woes of poverty and plainness, I thought I'd been signalled out to divine the future.

I remember thinking that if I could get away from Fountainville, I'd be able to reinvent my past and become a different person. I tried running away several times, never having the courage to get very far. Once, I put a knapsack on my back and managed to get out as far as the Northern Forest Ridge – ten kilometres out of town, past where Rafi's house stands in the forests of timber and mahogany.

I found out only later that Begum knew all along. She had deployed one of Kedar's men to shadow me. 'You were a stubborn thing,' she said. 'It was the only way to resolve it, to let you follow it through.'

I walked with such determination, up and down on those spindly wicket legs of mine, all through that jungle scrub, until I'd spent all my energy. When I had gone as far as I could, I sat on the forest floor and ate two pieces of bread and hard cheese, a handful of almonds and two peaches – all the food I'd carried with me. Then, just as stubbornly, I turned around and walked right back.

When I came home, all Begum said was, 'There you are then.'

I was disappointed. I had expected her to be in a state. But it was as if she hadn't even noticed I'd been missing. Of course, I couldn't have known that she knew. Begum always knew.

It's what she'll say when we go back to her now. 'There you are then.' As if there had never been any real danger of us disappearing.

EPILOGUE

How long did it take? It depends who you ask. All I know is that none of it was easy. Those initial years after Kedar was killed were the most difficult I've ever known. There was my own guilt of course, not dissimilar to what I felt after losing my family; a sense that I had instigated the entire chain of events by my refusal to do what was asked of me. By asserting myself, in other words.

Do I regret not climbing on the bus with my family? Or having had Owain's child even though I knew that nothing about our relationship would ever be *normal*? There are moments. Even now, surrounded by such happiness, such abundance, I cannot help but think how we failed Kedar by not foreseeing the danger to his life.

We did avenge his death eventually. Not in the way Begum would have preferred – with Marra's head on a pole. There was a war crimes tribunal instead, facilitated by Leo in the Mainland. During the weeks of the trial, the Prime Minister – a sheep of a man – squat, idiotic, nasal, who blinked every time he lied, kept appearing on television, talking about the 'magnificent political will' of the people of the Borderlands, about how a democratic nation, (they do *love* bandying that word around these days), can't afford to forget its less fortunate people.

The news channels spliced speeches of the Sheep-Man with scenes of Marra's jungle capture. It was gruesome. The way the army closed in on him. They called it 'Operation Forest Thunder' – after a movie of all things – one of those cheap action films they make on the Mainland. It was done in the same spirit of chest-beating chauvinism. God knows, I hold no candle to Marra, but to smoke out the villages like they did; to disrupt innocent people's lives; to use 500 soldiers including cavalry, artillery and air force – all to catch one man! It took two months to find him.

To drag him out of a hole in the ground where he barely had place to lie down! They lifted him out – bearded, soiled, utterly defeated.

All over the country people watched in a semi-hypnotised state, unable to separate reality from fantasy. On the Mainland, where we had always been viewed as footnotes to their own narrative, there was a reversal of sorts. We went from being invisible to exotic. Movie producers were already thinking of how to make us their next destination, the Tourist Board were designing luxury adventure holidays on one end of the spectrum and reality tours on the other. Ordinary Mainlanders, who had only ever viewed us as people who did their menial jobs for them, saw us for the first time, as dangerous – *These guys used to headhunt people, Don't piss them off!* In Fountainville and the rest of the Borderlands, people watched collectively in homes and bars and saloons, drunk on the idea of comeuppance.

We found it difficult to keep up with the unfolding events. It was hardest for Begum, who was no doubt forced to remember the long-ago time of her own jungle hideout experience; how Kedar saved her from Haroon Sherriff and kicked off the dramatic start of their thirty-five year love affair.

'Explain to me,' Begum said to Leo, who was watching the results of the trial with us, 'Is this considered humane? All this circus pandemonium, for what? To throw a man in a jail for the rest of his life? I don't understand. Nothing brings back the dead.'

★

We never reopened the clinic. There was no need to discuss it. We donated our equipment to the new hospital and converted the greenhouse into a shelter for single mothers, the destitute, and elders. Chanu Rose and Sabina are in charge of running it. We also began supporting the House of Hope, actively contributing to its many rehabilitation and outreach programmes. Earl and Mala travel with the volunteers, telling their own story of drug addiction and rehabilitation, which inspires current drug-users to join the programme.

The irony is that all our charity work was and continues to be funded by the success of La Saĝon de Fountainville — our ultra-chic health and wellness line, which is all the rage in cosmopolitan corners of the globe. It turns out that before disappearing into the den of Somaville, Owain had sent samples of Begum's potions to a friend who ran a weekly stall at a farmer's market. Our products did so well that within a few months of the stall's operation there were several business proposals to open a flagship store. All these proposals lay gathering dust in the pile of post that was waiting for Owain at the Sanity Boarding House. It was only after the long rehabilitation process that we found out that there were people across the seas who were desperate to know where to get hold of their next tub of *Neem Butter Nirvana*.

La Saĝon de Fountainville also supports and pays for our R&D laboratory where we work to increase sustainable productivity, conserve biodiversity, and develop regeneration options. The entire town's focus has shifted towards preserving our forests, and under

Leo's supervision, we're in the process of patenting all our traditional remedies.

For years, Begum talked about writing a memoir but she was too busy to actually write it. She wanted to tell the story of her life – how an ambitious woman from the Borderlands changed the course of her destiny. She thought it was movie material, full of adventure, intrigue, love, loss and redemption. She wanted to write about the breakdown of events after Kedar was murdered, and the long difficult arc of continuing to live without him. She wanted to re-examine the notion of the idealised nuclear family – to write about her inability to have children, the failures and short-sightedness of the surrogacy business, our tribal practices where child-rearing is a community effort, and how we gave all that up when the Baptists converted us. Most of all she wanted to write about how I entered her life, and how along with me came Rafi, Owain, Leo, Earl, Mala, Sabina, Chanu Rose and our children.

★

Having a child was exactly as I feared it would be. Full of love and constant anxiety. Jun is thinner than I would have hoped, and weak at sports, but he can talk up a storm, and is fearless. He has a joke and a story for everyone, and is remarkably unconcerned about the fact that he has four mothers and four fathers. The love of his life is his sister, Pearl, who was born a few hours after him, delivered by Dr Willis in Begum's front room.

Chanu Rose chose to keep Pearl and live with us. She was right about her husband. He'd been ready to put a hatchet in her head when he found out. He had spotted her on that infamous viral video, pregnant and clearly not studying to be a secretary. He blustered up to Begum's house with two of his cronies shouting and raving about the honour of his woman. There had never been any real danger, of course. Rafi could have swatted that pathetic triumvirate in a flash. But it was upsetting for Chanu Rose to have to listen to all their curses, to reflect on the many lost hours she'd wasted with that lummox.

What we've created, this new paradigm of family, seems so normal to us now, so effortless. Rafi and Sabina continue an on-off love affair. He spends most of his time in the forests but he comes to town once a week with his usual menagerie to pick up his supply of whisky. He's grown very fond of Mala's boy, Mingus. Now that the old chief is dead, Rafi has become Mingus's great protector, taking him out into the jungles and teaching him to identify different species of trees and insects.

Owain and Leo have built a beautiful wooden house at the foothills of the Northern Forest Ridge. We have our annual spring festival get-together here, which gets increasingly raucous as the years go by and the tiers of our extended family grow. Owain, who fancies himself as something of a landscape painter these days, spends more than half the year here, while Leo's visits are more sporadic. 'Someone's got to have a real job to support the artists,' he jokes. Leo brings with him all the excitement and energy of the spinning world, so naturally the children adore him best. Despite all the development and new-fangled technology, everything still feels slightly out of reach in Fountainville.

So much has changed, yet much remains the same. Main Street has swelled into greater chaos, but the old establishments like the Ambition Computer Centre and the Gloria Hallelujah are thriving. Mr Quintus sold the Sanity Boarding House to Mainlanders, who converted it into a chic B&B called *The Lady*. Pastor Joseph's successor, a fiery young man, Pastor Nelson, has been a great help to our cause by setting up temporary health camps, and by personally distributing condoms and sterile needles to those in need. 'God prefers you to abstain,' he tells them, 'But if you're going to do things, at least learn to protect yourself.'

When I walk around Fountainville I'm sometimes reminded of my ancient, persistent desire to leave it. I have had several opportunities over the years to travel, and it was always as marvellous as I dreamt: cities floating on water, kingdoms in the jungle, bridges and skyscrapers. The world is full of wonders. But I have always been happy to return home, to its particular combination of eucalyptus and pine, wood smoke and dirt. To sit under the giant alder tree and drink at the fountain.

The Lady of the Fountain
a synopsis

Arthur was in Caerllion ar Wysg with Gwenhyfar and his knights, Owain, Cynon and Cai. He asked them to tell stories while he slept. Cynon told of a journey he had taken in the remote and uninhabited regions of the world in search of a worthy opponent.

He told how he came to a beautiful valley and a plain with a castle. He was welcomed and inside he saw twenty-four beautiful maidens. While eating he explained his quest and was advised to travel on until he met a huge black-haired man with one foot and one eye, surrounded by animals, who would answer him rudely but tell him what to look for. Cynon did so and the black-haired man directed him to a valley with a great tree in the middle. Under the tree was a well and near the well a marble slab with a silver bowl fastened to it by a silver chain. He told Cynon to throw a bowlful of water across the slab, after which there would be a tremendous noise and a shower of hailstones which would nearly kill him and not leave one leaf on the tree. A flock of birds would land in the tree and sing, after which he would see a knight, all in black, approaching. Cynon did as he was told and was soundly beaten by the knight, returning home in disgrace.

Listening to him, Owain was keen to find the place, but Cynon laughed at him. At dawn the next day Owain slipped away on his horse and set out for the remote and desolate regions. He journeyed until he found the castle and valley, and he too was attacked by the black knight. Owain struck the knight a mortal blow and the knight fled towards a shining castle behind them. He was let in but the portcullis lowered, cutting Owain's horse in half as he followed, leaving him trapped between two gates.

Owain was in a quandary. A maiden with yellow hair approached and, liking him, gave him a ring which would make him invisible. She told him that when the men of the castle came to look for him, he should follow her. Owain did so and she took him to a beautiful upstairs room from where, the next day, he saw the mourning procession for the knight he had killed. Following the bier was a beautiful woman and he fell instantly in love. The maiden, Luned, told him this woman was the Lady of the Well, wife of the dead black knight, and that she would not love him. But still she went to her mistress and argued on his behalf, telling her she needed a knight from Arthur's court to help her defend the well. Eventually the Lady told her to go to Arthur's court and find such a knight, but Luned stayed in the room with Owain until it was time for her to return and then brought him to the Lady. The Lady recognised him as the knight who had killed her husband, but she took advice and called for bishops to marry them. Owain defended the well for three years, ransoming the knights who attacked and sharing the money with his barons so that everyone was happy.

Then Arthur, guided by Cynon and Cai, came to find Owain. When they came to the well Owain, dressed as a black knight, attacked them. But when they recognised him there was rejoicing and, after a feast of three months, the Lady of the Well allowed Owain to return to Britain for three months. Instead he stayed three years.

One day a maiden approached his table at Caerllion ar Wysg and grabbed his ring. 'This is what we do to a deceitful cheat and a traitor,' she said, and turned away.

Owain remembered his journey and grew sad. The next day he set out again for the remote regions of the world, wandering until he grew weak. Descending to a park he met a widowed countess whose maiden treated him with precious ointments until he was healed and defended the countess in return. Travelling on he heard shrieks from a forest. He saw a cleft rock with a snake in it and a pure white lion trying to escape. Owain killed the snake and the lion followed him. As he ate that evening Owain heard human groaning from nearby. He called out and was told it was Luned, imprisoned in stone because of a knight who had betrayed the Lady of the Well. She said he had to come to rescue her within two days or she would die. She directed Owain to a castle nearby where everyone was sad. The earl there told him his two sons had been captured by a monster who would kill them unless he exchanged them for his daughter. With the lion's help Owain killed the monster then returned to the field where Luned was about to be burned alive by two men. Again with the lion's help he rescued her and returned Luned to the Lady of the Well. He took the Lady to Arthur's court and she was his wife as long as she lived.

Then Owain and the lion came to the court of the Black Oppressor, who had imprisoned twenty-four maidens. They fought and the Black Oppressor begged for mercy, promising to run the house as a hostel for the weak and the strong if spared. Owain agreed and left the next day. Arthur greeted him joyfully and he was successful wherever he went.

Synopsis by Penny Thomas
for the full story see *The Mabinogion, A New Translation*
by Sioned Davies (Oxford World's Classics, 2007).

Afterword

I did not grow up reading the stories of the *Mabinogion*. My childhood was monopolised by the *Mahabharata* and the *Ramayana*, heroic epics involving gods, goddesses and many-headed demons, whose attributes were invoked daily, as if they weren't mythical characters at all, but people who lived and walked among us. In India, where I grew up, myths are everywhere; they are pervasive and alive in the most wonderful and frightening ways, and they survive in multiple retellings. We stake ownership in them because they inform our most basic ideas of vice and virtue. Myths are, ultimately, personal. And that's why I believe it's somewhat dangerous to meddle with other people's myths.

When I was asked to retell 'The Lady of the

Fountain,' I suffered all the usual outsider's misgivings. My Welsh connections are tenuous, after all. Whatever I know of Wales, I know from my mother. She was born in Nercwys, Flintshire, in 1947, and grew up speaking Welsh as her first language, although I can't remember her ever speaking it to us. The one Welsh word I know is *hiraeth*. My mother moved to India in 1968, and she must have felt a whole lot of *hiraeth* because the stories she told of Wales came to us in the form of memories. I had my own memories of course – summers in Nercwys, the beach in Rhyl, and later, as an adult, making my own discoveries in Abergavenny, the Brecon Beacons, and Carmarthenshire. But for the longest time, my picture of Wales had been pieced together from my mother's stories: a place of bluebells and primroses, coal-sheds and gooseberries, mountains, sheep, *bara brith* and netball.

Myths, like memories, are not constant. They are vague, changeable, geographically indeterminate, subsisting upon layers and layers of ever-shifting narrative. Myths, like memories, are often collective. It means that no matter how close we hold to them, they themselves don't accept boundaries. They are forever open, ready to be transformed and reinterpreted. For this reason, and perhaps, to tap into my latent Welshness, I agreed to enter the world of the *Mabinogion*, ready to take on all those, for me, unpronounceable Welsh names and fantastical Celtic happenings.

'The Lady of the Fountain' is a particularly strange tale, full of mirrors and multiplicities. Every time I read it, it offered me a new way in, and a new way out. One character enchanted me from the start – Luned, the Lady's handmaid. She had chutzpah and guile, and unlike the Lady herself, who is never named, and who has little to say, Luned dominates the tale. She is obstinate, pragmatic, steadfast in her devotion to Owain, and it is her relationship with the knight, not the Lady's, that seems the more authentic.

Owain, the ostensible hero of the story, is a perplexing character – not entirely chivalrous, but certainly a man who has something to prove. He travels to the 'remote and uninhabited regions of the world', looking for the Black Knight in order to kill him, an endeavour in which he is successful. And then, somewhat bizarrely, he takes on the role of the murdered man by becoming the Black Knight. He marries the man's widow, the Lady of the Fountain, and agrees to protect her and her lands. All goes well until King Arthur and his retinue set out to find him, and when they do, they persuade Owain to come back to court for three months. The Lady gives her permission, and Owain stays away three years instead, too busy with his drinking companions to remember his duties as the Black Knight. And that's when the weird stuff really kicks in.

Wilderness, amnesia, a widowed countess, a white lion, a serpent, a mountain ogre, an incredibly sad Earl, and Luned, imprisoned in a stone vessel, all make an appearance in the latter half of the story. Owain's second journey to the remote regions of the world is in many ways, a mirror of the first, with several repeat characters and situations. Except that where the first journey is paradisiacal with its canter through picturesque valleys and the beguiling castle of twenty-four golden-haired maidens, the second journey, by contrast, is hellish – an underworld of madness, which the hero must brave through in order to redeem himself.

Which brings us to the unsettling conclusion of the story. Owain saves Luned from the wall of stone with the help of a white lion, and returns to the Lady of the Fountain for what seems like a millisecond before the entire jamboree abandons the fountain and follows Owain back to King Arthur's Court. After this happily ever after, there's also the addendum tale of the Black Oppressor, who has imprisoned twenty-four (the recurring number) beautiful and sad ladies, all of them daughters of earls. Naturally, Owain gets the better of him, frees the ladies, and brings them to court as well!

I call it an unsettling conclusion because throughout the story I had a sense that the fountain was important, that it was worth protecting. The fountain was, in a way, the central character – mysterious, magical, rooting the myth to a particular landscape. People were killed and maimed because of this fountain. The Lady was famous because of this fountain.

We never know exactly why it's so special, but we know it is. So it is something of an anticlimax when the fountain is so unceremoniously renounced. Still, it gave me a beginning. I knew that in my version, the fountain's keepers would remain loyal, that no amount of luring from distant lands could unsteady them.

★

Stories, for me, often begin with images. Images act as triggers to certain moods or situations, and can set the entire narrative arc in motion. What stayed with me from the original myth were the fountain, the character of Luned, and the image of twenty-four golden-haired maidens, who seemed quite content to be captive in a castle. These women were like extras in a movie, body-doubles. They existed only as a collective, never individually, their main occupation in life apparently, to embroider, sow, and impress their great beauty upon passing strangers.

During the time I was reading 'The Lady of the

Fountain', I came across an article about the surrogacy business in India – a $2.3 billion industry fuelled by 350 fertility clinics, all relying on the services of poor, often illiterate women, who offered their 'wombs for rent' to mostly western clients. In America, where surrogacy is legal, the process can cost anywhere between $50,000-$100,000. In India, clinics charge between $15,000-$20,000, which includes the surrogate mother's fees of approximately $5,000 for her efforts. One of the doctors interviewed said of the current situation, 'When it comes to ethical conduct, it might as well be the Wild West. Forget laws... there are no rules.'

The article in question, 'Inside India's Rent-a-Womb Business', was printed with a photograph of a group of women in a room, lounging around in nighties, sitting or sleeping on a row of metal beds. The room was bare except for a wall-fan, a sagging curtain, and a clock. For the entire duration of their pregnancy, these women would stay in this 'cloistered' residential facility. Here then, was my castle of twenty-four maidens.

There were other inspirations: A trip I made with Médecins Sans Frontières to Nagaland, in the Northeast of India, to report on their healthcare situation (in a word – terrifying); and the American television series, *Deadwood*, a western set in the late 1800s in South Dakota at the height of the Gold Rush.

Deadwood helped to provide an interesting ethical framework for my story. To liken the surrogacy business to the Wild West, as the doctor in the article suggested, meant looking at those age-old motivations of money and greed; and how when there's an obscene amount of money to be made, various inelegant aspects of human behaviour are forced to the front. But Nagaland, a frontier land in its own right, offered most of the topographical and anthropological details for my imaginary town, Fountainville.

Nagaland is one of the most militarised zones in India with problems of drugs, arms and child trafficking. The tribes there used to be headhunters before being converted to Christianity by Baptists in the early1900s. Located in the tri-junction of India, China and Burma, Nagaland is not an easy place to get to. The mountains are stunning, and the surrounding forests are lush and filled with possible enchantments, but the roads are treacherous, sullied with potholes, hairpin bends and dizzying drops. Going to Nagaland was my experience of 'the remote and uninhabited regions of the world.'

The town of Mon, where I stayed, has a Main Street very much like the one in Fountainville, with an Ambition Computer Centre and a Sanity Boarding Home. The civic hospital, where I spent most of my time, was best described by a local as a 'glorified cowshed', with no running water, erratic electricity, dirty pea-green walls, and rickety iron beds with crumbling foam mattresses. The local staff, including doctors and nurses, all constantly chewed betel – a Naga preoccupation. Most of the cases treated at the hospital were for gunshot wounds (often alcohol-fuelled and self-inflicted while hunting for birds), electric shocks and pregnancy deliveries (although they had no facilities for C-sections). The nearest big hospital was a ten-hour drive away. Compared to the sophisticated medical facilities found in mainland

India, Nagaland was stuck in a time warp circa the age of Florence Nightingale.

When I began writing *Fountainville* I knew I didn't want to write a story about a place that already existed. The original myth is so wonderfully unspecific in its geography that it allowed me the rare freedom of writing about anywhere. Certainly, Nagaland is present, as are echoes of the Wild West with the gambling saloons, opium dens and gun slinging, but it is the fountain and all its possibilities that really centre my story.

★

The great Indian poet and scholar AK Ramanujan had an interesting theory about time in myths. In male-centric myths, he wrote, the prince goes off on adventures and conquests, and this is how time is measured. But in female-centric myths, time is calculated between the interior and the exterior.

Some of the themes I was keen to explore in 'The Lady of the Fountain' were the idea of portents and signs, the Matryoshka effect of the story within the story within the story, visibility and invisibility, the body and sexuality, and the tensions between the insider and the outsider. Very early on I knew that my retelling of the myth would have to be female-centric, not least because the fountain is a fundamentally feminine symbol. Wells in all mythologies, but particularly Celtic wells, are receptacles of healing and fertility, the place where the natural and supernatural worlds connect. Inner-outer. They are sources of water, that most important of the elements – life giving, sacred.

I knew as well that I would have to give agency to the two main female characters – Luned and the Lady, or in my version, Luna and Begum. For agency, they would need to have strong voices and strong desires. To shift the story so decisively towards this inner-outer model meant greatly diminishing the swashbuckling ways of the knight, our hero, but I compensated him with an inner-outer experience of his own, I hope.

Retelling a myth can be a challenging experience.

Retelling a myth that is not your own, doubly so. One of the privileges of writing fiction is that you are allowed to manipulate reality and imagination in order to fashion your own sense of the truth. I made several departures from 'The Lady of the Fountain' in order to restore a unity that I felt lacking in the original, which I hope will not be taken amiss. There were so many possible stories to tell. For a while I did not know whether I wanted to write about a lion escaped from a circus, or a wish-giving well in a French village during WWII. Like all stories thankfully, *Fountainville* proved to have a pioneering spirit of its own.

Tishani Doshi

Acknowledgements

Thanks are due to Carlo Pizzati, Michael Wiegers, Diane Paragas and Arpana Agarwal for early inspiration; DW Gibson at Ledig House for the usual; Scott Carney for his reportage on surrogacy; Marina Berdini at Médecins Sans Frontières for sending me to Nagaland; and Penny Thomas at Seren for asking.

NEW STORIES FROM THE
MABINOGION

OWEN SHEERS: WHITE RAVENS

Two stories, two different times, but the thread of an ancient tale runs through the lives of twenty-first-century farmer's daughter Rhian and the mysterious Branwen... Wounded in Italy, Matthew O'Connell is seeing out WWII in a secret government department spreading rumours and myths to the enemy. But when he's given the task of escorting a box containing six raven chicks from a remote hill farm in Wales to the Tower of London, he becomes part of a story over which he seems to have no control.

RUSSELL CELYN JONES: THE NINTH WAVE

Pwyll, a young Welsh ruler in a post-oil world, finds his inherited status hard to take. And he's never quite sure how he's drawn into murdering his future wife's fiancé, losing his only son and switching beds with the king of the underworld. In this bizarrely upside-down, medieval world of the near future, life is cheap and the surf is amazing; but you need a horse to get home again down the M4.

GWYNETH LEWIS: THE MEAT TREE

A dangerous tale of desire, DNA, incest and flowers plays out within the wreckage of an ancient spaceship in *The Meat Tree*, an absorbing retelling of one of the best-known Welsh myths by prizewinning writer and poet, Gwyneth Lewis.

An elderly investigator and his female apprentice hope to extract the fate of the ship's crew from its antiquated virtual reality game system, but their empirical approach falters as the story tangles with their own imagination.

NEW STORIES FROM THE
MABINOGION

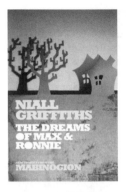

NIALL GRIFFITHS: THE DREAMS OF MAX & RONNIE

There's war and carnage abroad and Iraq-bound squaddie Ronnie is out with his mates 'forgetting what has yet to happen'. He takes something dodgy and falls asleep for three nights in a filthy hovel where he has the strangest of dreams, watching the tattooed tribes of modern Britain surrounding a grinning man playing war games.

Meanwhile gangsta Max is fed up with life in Cardiff nightclub, Rome, and chases a vision of the perfect woman in far-flung parts of his country. As Max loses his heart, his followers fear he's losing his touch.

FFLUR DAFYDD: THE WHITE TRAIL

Life is tough for Cilydd after his heavily pregnant wife vanishes in a supermarket one wintry afternoon. And his private-eye cousin Arthur doesn't appear to be helping much.

The trail leads them to a pigsty, a cliff edge and a bloody warning that Cilydd must never marry again. But eventually the unlikely hero finds himself on a new and dangerous quest – a hunt for the son he never knew, a meeting with a beautiful and mysterious girl, and a glimpse inside the House of the Missing.

HORATIO CLARE: THE PRINCE'S PEN

The Invaders' drones hear all and see all, and England is now a defeated archipelago, but somewhere in the high ground of the far west, insurrection is brewing.

Ludo and Levello, the bandit kings of Wales, call themselves freedom fighters. Levello has the heart and help of Uzma, from Pakistan – the only other country in the free world. Ludo has a secret, lethal if revealed.

NEW STORIES FROM THE
MABINOGION

LLOYD JONES: SEE HOW THEY RUN

Small-minded academic Dr Llwyd McNamara has a grant to research Wales' biggest hero, rugby star Dylan Manawydan Jones – Big M. But as the doctor plays with USB sticks in his office, the gods have other plans...

Llwyd discovers a link between Big M and his own life at the luxurious but strange Hotel Corvo. But from here things only get stranger. Are claims to a link between Big M and the Celtic myths of the past just a load of academic waffle... and what is the significance of the mouse tattoo?

CYNAN JONES: BIRD, BLOOD, SNOW

"No matter how you build them, the world will come crashing against your fences."

Hoping to give him a better start, Peredur's mother takes him from the estates. But when local kids cycle into his life he heads after them, accompanied by the notion of finding Arthur – an absent, imaginary guardian. Used to making up his own worlds, he's something of a joke. Until he seriously maims one of the older kids. And that's when the trouble starts.

TREZZA AZZOPARDI: THE TIP OF MY TONGUE

Enid wants a dog and she wants to be a spy, but listening in on adult conversations doesn't seem to bring her any nearer to understanding their troubled world. For all that, when times get tough and she has to stay with the Erbins, particularly her rich and spoilt cousin Geraint, she has plenty of verbal ammunition to help her fight her corner.

The original Enid warns her misguided husband of approaching villains, even though he has forbidden her to speak. Trezza Azzopardi's young Enid is also unlikely to respect a gagging order.